BEFORE HE HUNTS

(A MACKENZIE WHITE MYSTERY—BOOK 8)

BLAKE PIERCE

BOOKS BY BLAKE PIERCE

RILEY PAIGE MYSTERY SERIES

MACKENZIE WHITE MYSTERY SERIES

AVERY BLACK MYSTERY SERIES

KERI LOCKE MYSTERY SERIES

CHAPTER ONE

The plane was taking her to Nebraska.

Mackenzie blinked, unable to shake the thought from her mind.

She usually had no problem falling asleep on a plane. But this flight was different. She felt like there was something out west that was literally pulling the plane toward it like a magnet. And she would not be returning to Washington, DC, until she had solved a current case that reached nearly twenty years into her past— pointing at the death of her father.

It was a case that had been calling her for years. She'd gone above and beyond to prove herself, and McGrath was finally setting her loose on this case. It was no longer just about the unsolved murder of her father seventeen years ago; similar murders were occurring now, all connected by a mysterious clue that no one had yet deciphered. Business cards featuring the nonexistent business name of Barker Antiques.

Mackenzie thought about those business cards as she looked out the window. The afternoon sky was clear. Beyond the scattering of plump white clouds, she could just barely catch sight of the vein-like structure of roadways that carved through the Midwest down below. Nebraska was close now, its cornfields and flat expanses looming about forty-five minutes ahead.

"You okay?"

She blinked and looked away from the window, turning to her right. Ellington sat in the seat next to her. She knew he was nervous, too. He knew how much this case meant to her and was putting unnecessary pressure on himself. Even now, he was nervously picking at the lid of the cup that had held ginger ale ten minutes ago.

"Yeah, I'm good," she said. "If I'm being honest, I can't wait to get started."

"You got a plan in mind?" he asked.

"I do," she said.

As she wound her way through her plan of attack, she realized that this was one of the reasons she had fallen in love with him. He could tell that she needed to talk through it all but would shut down if he asked her point-blank. So instead of asking about her

1

emotional state, he used the façade of work to pry. She was on to his tricks, but that was okay. He knew how to work around her defenses in a way that was charming and caring.

So she discussed her plan of attack. It all started by meeting with the local PD and the small team of FBI agents that had been working the case. She also planned to bring Kirk Peterson, the private detective who had worked the case for a while, in on it. Although he had been in a miserable state the last time she had seen him, he had the most insight to offer.

From there, she wanted to find and speak with a man named Dennis Parks. His fingerprints had been found on Gabriel Hambry, a man who had been strategically set up as a red herring a week ago. She was well aware that Parks could also be another red herring, but the fact that Dennis Parks had once known her father made it all the more appealing. The connection was a small one—a mutual acquaintance as Parks had served as a police officer for one year before calling it quits and getting into real estate.

Her father, after all, seemed to be the first victim in a string of seemingly random murders that had been spread over nearly two decades.

After meeting with Dennis Parks, she wanted to meet with the family of a man who had been killed several months ago—a man named Jimmy Scotts. Scotts had died in an almost identical fashion as her father and had been the murder that had effectively reopened her father's case.

She stopped her plans there although she knew there was more to it. But it was something she was not ready to contend with yet—much less verbalize in front of Ellington.

At some point, she was going to have to face her past. She'd been there before, tiptoeing through the house where she grew up. But it had been fleeting. At the time she had not realized it, but it had terrified her. It was like willingly walking into a house you knew to be haunted, locking yourself inside, and then throwing away the key.

She'd have to face it this time around. It was hard enough to admit that to herself without wondering what Ellington would think of it.

He nodded in all the right parts as she carried him through her step-by-step approach. They'd briefly discussed their roles in a meeting with McGrath as they had booked the trip to Nebraska. One element to the seemingly multilayered case was the recent murder of vagrants. The body count was now up to four, each body left with one of the Barker Antiques business cards. Ellington had volunteered to do his best to get that end of the case in order while Mackenzie stayed closer to the core of the case—the deaths of her father and Jimmy Scotts, and the more recent death of Gabriel Hambry.

"You know," Ellington said when she was done, "if we can wrap this one up, I think your career in DC might hit the stratosphere. You're already one of the better field agents the bureau has. I hope you like dealing with bureaucratic bullshit and sitting behind a desk. Because that's what a stellar record with the bureau gets you."

"Is that so?" she asked. "Then why aren't you parked behind a desk yet?"

He smirked at her. "That stings, White."

He reached out and took her hand. She could feel tension in his grip but there was the usual degree of comfort at his touch as well.

She was grateful that he was with her. While she was usually all for tackling things on her own, even she had to admit that she was going to need the moral and emotional support that only Ellington could provide if she had any hope of wrapping this case up.

She held onto his hand as the Midwest continued to roll by beneath them. Nebraska drew closer and closer, the plane pulled on by that magnetic hold that Mackenzie's past seemed to have over her.

CHAPTER TWO

The Omaha field office was pleasant to the eye. It was smaller than the headquarters in DC, meaning there was less chatter. There was also not the tension of something always on the brink of happening, a trait that the offices in DC were usually rife with. The place felt calming.

As they were signing in at the front desk, Mackenzie noticed a man headed directly for them. He was walking with purpose, a thin smile on his face. His face was familiar but she could not for the life of her recall the man's name.

"Agent White, it's great to see you again," the man said as he approached. He was roughly six feet tall and carried himself well. He was rather slim but still intimidating looking. His slicked back black hair made him look a bit older than he probably was.

"Likewise," she said, shaking the hand he extended to her.

She was thankful that Ellington remembered his name, using it as the two men greeted one another. "Agent Penbrook," he said. "Great to see you."

She then remembered; Agent Darren Penbrook had been the lead on the case when she had flown out in the hopes of arresting Gabriel Hambry—only to find out within less than an hour that he had been killed.

"Come with me," Penbrook said. "There won't be much of a meeting, but there are a few details I think you guys should be caught up on…some of which are fairly recent."

"How recent?" Mackenzie asked.

"Within the last twenty-four hours."

Mackenzie knew how things worked at most levels within the bureau and assumed they were no different in Omaha than they were in DC. There was no use asking questions in that moment. So during the elevator ride to the second floor and a quick jaunt through a hallway that led to a blocked-off conference room, the three of them passed the time with small talk: the flight, the weather, how busy things stayed in DC.

But those niceties were dashed the moment Penbrook took them into the conference room. He closed the door behind them, leaving the three of them in the large room with an elegant and finely polished conference table. There was already a projector set up and ready to go in the center of the table.

"So what sort of updates were you referring to?" Mackenzie asked.

"Well, you know about the fourth murdered vagrant, right?" he asked.

"Yes. It happened yesterday, right? Sometime in the afternoon?"

"That's right," Penbrook said. "He was killed with the same model of gun the others were killed with. This time, though, the killer had placed the business card between the victim's lips. We had the card tested and there were no fingerprints. The vagrant wasn't a local. His last known address was in California and that was four years ago. Looking for family members or people he worked with has turned into nothing but a ghost hunt. And that's been the case with most of these vagrants. We did, however, find his brother. He's also a vagrant and according to his reports, might be slightly delusional."

"Is there anything else?" Ellington asked.

"Yes. And this one really sucks. It's actually thrown us for a loop and is currently where the case is stuck at the moment. You recall the fingerprints we got off of Gabriel Hambry's body, correct?"

"Yes," Mackenzie said. "They belonged to a man named Dennis Parks—a man who had a history with my father."

"Exactly. Sounded like a promising lead, right?"

"I take it the lead fell through?" Mackenzie asked.

"It never had a chance. Dennis Parks was found dead in his bed this morning. Shot in the back of the head. His wife was also killed. From what we can tell, she was also killed while in the bed but her body was moved to the couch."

Both Penbrook and Ellington looked in Mackenzie's direction. She knew what they were thinking. *The killer set it up to look like the scene at Jimmy Scotts's murder...like my father's murder.*

Penbrook took this moment to show a slide from the crime scene. It was of Dennis Parks, face down in bed with the back of his head blown out. The positioning of it was almost too eerie for Mackenzie. Had she not known the identity of the victim, she could have easily thought she was looking at a photo from her father's crime scene all those years ago.

The slide then shifted to an image of the wife. She was on the couch, her dead eyes staring slightly upward. There was dried blood on the side of her face.

"Was there a business card at the scene?" Mackenzie asked.

"Yes," Penbrook replied. "On the nightstand. And, just so you can get the scope of it all, here's a shot from the latest vagrant scene."

He changed slides and Mackenzie found herself looking at a man lying on a city sidewalk. The side of his head was a bloody mess, contrasted almost too perfectly with the white business card that had been partially shoved between his lips.

"It seems like the killer is just having fun at this point," Ellington said. "That's messed up."

He was right. Mackenzie was sure that there was an almost playful nature to the way the card had been placed in the victim's mouth. Add that to the fact that the killer was also apparently placing fingerprints on the cards and other victims to lead them to red herrings and that meant you had a determined, smart, and morbid killer.

He thinks he's being funny here, she thought as she looked to the picture of the victim.

"So why is he choosing vagrants to kill?" Mackenzie asked. "If he's coming back to kill more so long after having killed my father, why the homeless? And is there any connection between these vagrants and Jimmy Scotts or Gabriel Hambry?"

"None that we have found," Penbrook said.

"So maybe he's just rubbing our noses in it," Mackenzie said. "Maybe he knows the deaths of vagrants aren't going to be as high of a priority as if he were killing everyday citizens. And if that's the case, he really is doing this as an almost playful act."

"That about the vagrant community," Ellington said. "If we ask around, do you think we might get some sort of information from other vagrants in the area?"

"Oh, we've tried," Penbrook said. "But they won't talk. They're afraid whoever is doing the killing will come after them next if they speak up."

"We need to talk to the brother of the latest victim," Mackenzie said. "Any idea where he might be? Does he live around here?"

"Sort of," Penbrook said. "Like his brother, he's living on the streets. Well, he *was.* He's at a correctional facility right now. Can't remember what for, but maybe public intoxication. His record is filled with little misdemeanors that put him in prison for a week or two at a time. It happens a lot, you know. Some of them do it just to get free housing for a few days."

"You have any problems with us going to see him?" Mackenzie asked.

"Not at all," Penbrook said. "I'll have someone make a call and let them know you're coming."

"Thanks."

"I feel like I should be thanking you," Penbrook said. "We're excited to finally have you out here working on this thing."

Finally, she thought. She said nothing, though, and left it at that.

Because the truth was, she was excited, too. She was excited to finally have the opportunity to wrap up a truly bizarre case that reached all the way back into her childhood and pointed directly back to her father.

CHAPTER THREE

Delcroix Correctional Facility was tucked back off of the highway on a patch of land that was bland and featureless. It was the only building on a strip of about five hundred acres of land—not quite a prison per se, but certainly not somewhere a standard person off of the street would want to spend any significant amount of time.

Mackenzie and Ellington were waved through the small security partition at the entrance and directed to park in the employee lot on the back end of the property. From there, they were checked in at the main security check-in and ushered into a small waiting area where there was already a woman waiting for them.

"Agents White and Ellington?" she asked.

Mackenzie shook her hand first as introductions were made. The woman's name was Mel Kellerman. She was fairly short and slightly overweight yet had the demeanor of a woman who had seen hard time and laughed in its face.

As Kellerman led them out of the waiting area, she gave a brief rundown of the place.

"I serve as Security Administrator," she said. "As such, I can tell you that the man you're here to see poses no threat. His name is Bryan Taylor. Fifty years old and a recovering heroin addict. He sometimes has conversations with people that aren't there. His record is minor but he stays on our radar because this is the fourth small-time crime he's committed in the last year. We think it's just to get free room and board."

"And what was his latest crime?" Mackenzie asked.

"He took a piss on the back tire of a city bus in broad daylight."

Ellington chuckled. "Was he drunk?"

"Nope," Kellerman said. "Just said he really needed to take a piss."

She led them down a small hall and then down an even smaller corridor. At the end, they came to a door which Kellerman opened for them. The room contained only a table and five chairs. A disheveled-looking man occupied one of the chairs while a man in a security uniform occupied another. The guard turned as they came in and got up from his seat right away.

8

"Is Mr. Taylor giving you any problems?" Kellerman asked the guard.

"No. He's on a rant, though. The Russians and Trump again."

"Ah, one of my favorites," Kellerman said. She turned to Mackenzie and Ellington. "I'll be one room over if you need me. But I think you'll be okay."

With that, Kellerman and the other guard exited the room, leaving them with Bryan Taylor.

"Hello, Mr. Taylor," Mackenzie said as she took a seat across the table from him. "Did they tell you why we were coming?"

Taylor nodded his head sadly. "Yeah. You want to know about my brother—how he died."

"That's right," Mackenzie said. "I'm sorry for your loss."

Taylor only shrugged. He was drumming his fingers on the table and looked back and forth between Mackenzie and Ellington.

"Well, I'm Agent White and this is my partner, Agent Ellington," Mackenzie said.

"Yeah, I know. From the FBI." He rolled his eyes when he said this.

"Mr. Taylor...tell me...did your brother have any enemies? Any people that might have something against him?"

Taylor barely even thought about it before answering. "Nope. Just our momma, and she's been dead for seven years now."

"Were you close with your brother?"

"We weren't best friends or anything like that," Taylor said. "But we got along well enough. He hung out with some shady fuckers, though. Illuminati types. I honestly wasn't too surprised to hear he died. Those Illuminati creeps have something against the homeless. The famous, too. You know they killed Kennedy, right?"

"I heard that," Ellington said, barely able to contain his smirk.

Mackenzie stepped on his foot under the table and did her best to forge on.

"Have you had any other friends that were murdered recently?" she asked.

"I don't think so. But I don't really hang with the same crowd very often. On the streets, more friends just means more people to rip you off."

"Just one more question, Mr. Taylor," Mackenzie said. "Have you ever heard of a business called Barker Antiques?"

He didn't think very long about this answer, either. "Nope. Can't say that I have. Never stepped foot into an antiques shop. I don't have cash to be dropping on old dusty relics. Crazy-ass rich people run places like that. Shop there, too."

Mackenzie nodded and let out a little sigh. "Well, thank you for your time and cooperation, Mr. Taylor. I do ask that if you think of anything else about your brother that might help us figure out who might have killed him, please let someone that works here know so they can get the information to us."

"Oh yeah, I will. You know…you might head out to Nevada. I bet there are some answers there."

"Nevada?" Mackenzie asked. "Why's that?"

"Area 51. Groom Lake. It's not the Illuminati, but everyone knows those top secret government places have been nabbing homeless folks for ages. They run experiments and tests on them out there in the desert."

Mackenzie turned away before Taylor could see her hesitant grin. Based on what she knew about him, she knew he couldn't help it—that he was a few bricks short of a load. Ellington, on the other hand, was not able to remain quite as professional.

"Good tip, Mr. Taylor. We'll certainly look into that."

As they reached the exit, Mackenzie nudged him and leaned in close enough to whisper. "That was borderline mean," she said.

"How do you figure? I was just trying to make him feel like he had legitimately contributed to the investigation."

"You're going to hell," she said, smiling.

"Oh, I know. Down with all the Illuminati for sure."

***

As they headed back to their car, Mackenzie had already started to piece together their next step. It felt solid, yet at the same time, she could also understand why it was an avenue that had not been properly explored by the bureau yet.

"You know, Taylor *did* make one good point," Mackenzie said.

"Yeah?" Ellington asked. "I must have missed it."

"He talked about how some of those homeless communities are pretty tight. I think the bureau has been so concerned with how the vagrants might be connected to one another that they failed to seriously consider how people like Jimmy Scotts and Gabriel Hambry might be connected to them."

They got into the car, Ellington opting to take the driver's seat this time. "Ah, but that's not true. Homeless shelters and soup kitchens were contacted to see if either man had any affiliation with those kinds of places."

"Exactly," Mackenzie said. "It was assumed that they would have been connected to the vagrants in a way that had them *over* the vagrants. Maybe there's something else there."

"Like what? You think Scotts and Hambry might have been homeless at one point?"

"No idea. But let's say they *were*. That gives enough of a connection and would tell us that this guy is, for some reason or another, going after vagrants only."

"It's worth considering," Ellington said. "But that leaves one very important question: *why?*"

"Well, first, let's make sure I'm not getting too far ahead of myself."

"How?"

"From what I read in the reports, Gabriel Hambry has no next of kin. The only family he had left around are a set of grandparents that live in Maine. But Jimmy Scotts has a wife and two kids in Lincoln."

"And you want to head out that way?" Ellington asked.

"Well, considering the place I want to go after that is over six hours away, yeah…I think we should start there."

"Six hours away? Where the hell do you want to go? The other side of the state?"

"Yes, in fact. Morrill County. A little town called Belton."

"What's there?"

Having to suppress a little shiver, Mackenzie answered: "My past."

CHAPTER FOUR

They spent the drive to Lincoln going back and forth on possible theories. Why kill vagrants? Why wait so long to start killing again? Why Ben White, Mackenzie's father? Were there others before Ben White who had simply not been discovered?

There were far too many questions and basically zero answers. And while Mackenzie usually hated to speculate, it was sometimes the only tool to use when the real world offered you nothing. It seemed even more necessary now that she was back in Nebraska. It was a deceptively large state and without solid leads, speculation was all they had to go on.

Well, there was *one* lead but it seemed to be a phantom: business cards with the name of a nonexistent business on it. Which did them no good.

Mackenzie kept thinking about the business card as they made their way to Lincoln. It had to serve *some* purpose, even if it was nothing more than some elaborate riddle that the killer was asking them to unravel. She knew that there were a few people back in DC who had been consistently trying to crack such a code (if there was indeed one to be cracked) but they had come up with nothing so far.

The business cards on each body so far only pointed to one teasing conclusion: the killer *wanted* them to know each murder was his work. He wanted the authorities to keep count, to know what he was responsible for. It spoke of a killer who took pride not only in what he was doing, but also in the fact that he was sending the FBI in circles trying to find him.

This frustration was ripe in Mackenzie's mind as Ellington parked their car in front of the Scotts residence. They lived in an upper-middle-class home in the kind of neighborhood where all of the houses were built to resemble one another. The lawns were trimmed perfectly, and even as they got out of the car and headed for the Scotts's front door, Mackenzie spotted two dogs being walked by masters that were busy scrolling through their phones while they walked.

Based on the case files, Mackenzie knew the basics about Jimmy Scotts's wife, Kim. She worked from home as a technical writer for a software company and her kids were at school every day until 3:45. She had moved to Lincoln a month after Jimmy's death, stating that everything about Morrill County was nothing more than a devastating reminder of the life she had once lived with her husband.

It was 3:07 when Mackenzie knocked on the door. She'd love to be in and out without having to drag the kids through conversations and memories of their deceased father. According to the reports, the oldest of the two girls, a promising junior in high school, had taken the death especially hard.

A strikingly pretty middle-aged woman answered the door. She looked confused at first but then, perhaps after she took in their attire, seemed to understand who was on her doorstep and why they were there.

She frowned a bit before asking: "Can I help you?"

"I'm Agent White, and this is Agent Ellington, with the FBI," Mackenzie said. "I do apologize, but we were hoping you might be able to answer a few questions about your husband."

"Seriously?" Kim Scotts asked. "I've put this behind me. So have my daughters. I'd really rather not head back down that road if it can be helped. So thank you, but no."

She started to close the door on them but Mackenzie held out a hand. She stopped the door from closing, but not using much force.

"I understand that you've done your best to put it all behind you," she said. "Unfortunately, the killer has not. He's killed at least five others since your husband was killed." She nearly included the fact that there was a good chance that the killer had also killed her father nearly twenty years ago but decided to keep it to herself.

Kim Scotts opened her door back up. Instead of inviting them inside, though, she came out onto the porch. Mackenzie had seen this approach before. Kim was choosing to keep any and all conversation about her dead husband outside of the four walls of her home.

"So what do you think I can offer?" Kim asked. "I went through this at least three times after Jimmy died. I don't have any new information."

"Well, the bureau does," Mackenzie said. "For starters, after your husband and one other man, it appears that the killer took an interest in vagrants. He's killed four that we know of so far. Do you know of any connections Jimmy might have had with the homeless community?"

The question apparently baffled her. The expression on her face was one of confusion and annoyance. "No. The closest he would have come to being involved with the homeless was taking the

13

clothes he had grown tired of to the Salvation Army. We do that twice a year to free up closet space."

"What about people he worked with? Do you know if any of them might have had connections with homeless people or maybe even just those in dire need?"

"Doubtful. It was just him and two other guys that ran a small marketing company. Don't get me wrong…Jimmy was always a compassionate guy but he—neither of us, for that matter, ever really got into community involvement."

Mackenzie searched and searched for her next question but it would not come to her. She was now fairly confident that Jimmy Scotts had been randomly targeted. No reason, no motive, just the unfortunate luck to have been seen and apparently followed by the killer. This also made her think that maybe the deaths of Gabriel Hambry, Dennis Parks, and her father were also random.

Well, maybe not. There's a connection between my dad and Dennis Parks. So if they aren't random, why would the others be?

"What about your daughters?" Ellington asked, picking up the thread. "Are they perhaps involved in some sort of community outreach projects at school or something?"

"No," Kim said. The look on her face made it clear that she did not like viewing her daughters in light of this killer at all.

"You mentioned that your husband worked with a few friends at a marketing company. Do you know if they ever had any clients that might have been tied to some sort of community outreach?"

"That I don't know. If they did, it would have been a small project. Jimmy only ever talked about the big projects. But if you like, I have copies of all of their invoices. Somehow all of that came to me when he died. I can get them for you if you like."

"That would be helpful," Mackenzie said.

"One moment, please," Kim said. She walked back inside, closing the door behind her and still not inviting them in.

"Good call on the clients," Ellington said. "You think anything will come of it?"

She shrugged. "It can't hurt."

"That could be a lot of digging," he pointed out.

"Yeah. But that will give us something to do on that six-hour drive out to Morrill County."

"Fun."

Kim came back out onto the porch with five large folders all stacked together and held in place with binders and a huge rubber band. "Honestly," she said, "I'm glad to get rid of it. But if it's not asking too much, could you let me know if you find anything? I might have tried putting his death behind me, but that doesn't mean the mystery of it all doesn't drive me nuts sometimes."

"Absolutely," Mackenzie said. "Mrs. Scotts, thank you for your time and cooperation."

Kim gave them both a brief nod and stood there as they made their way back down the steps and toward the car. Mackenzie could feel the widow's eyes on her, making sure no mention of her deceased husband made it inside her house. Kim did not relax her posture until both Mackenzie and Ellington were in the car.

"Poor woman," Ellington said. "You think she's really moved on?"

"Maybe. She *says* she's moved on but she wasn't about to let us into her house. She didn't want mention of his death in there."

"But at the same time," he said, hefting the folders she'd handed them, "she seemed pleased to be rid of these."

"Maybe she also wants to remove reminders of him from the house, too," she said.

They pulled away from the house, the car pointed in the direction of the interstate. They were both quiet, almost in a respectful silence of the grieving widow they had just spoken to.

***

They were back at the field office just as the nine-to-five workers were packing up for the day. Mackenzie wondered what it was like to have a clock command your time rather than the pressing worries that came with the sordid cases she often found herself tasked with. She didn't think she'd be able to handle it.

She and Ellington met up with Penbrook in the same conference room they had visited that morning. It had been a long day, the early flight out of DC making it an early one, too. But knowing the next step in their process, Mackenzie found herself energized and ready to get moving again.

They filled Penbrook in on their talk with Kim Scotts and took some time to read through the invoices she had given them. It was done quickly, almost as an obligatory sort of exercise.

"What about here on the home front?" Ellington asked. "Any developments?"

"None," Penbrook said. "Quite honestly, I'd love to hear what you two have. I understand this case is close to you, Agent White. What's our next step?"

"I want to go out to Morrill County. It's where my father and Jimmy Scotts were both killed. And since my father's death seems to have been the first in this line, I think that's the best place to start."

"Looking for what, exactly?" Penbrook asked.

"I don't know yet."

"But don't let that fool you," Ellington told him. "She gets some of her best results when she goes in without a clue to what she's looking for."

She cut him a sly smile and returned her attention back to Penbrook. "I grew up in a town called Belton. I'm going to start there. I'll know the next step when it presents itself."

"If that's what you want to do, I won't try to dissuade you," Penbrook said. "But Morrill County is what…like six hours away?"

"I don't mind the driving," she said. "It'll be fine."

"When will you leave?"

"Maybe soon. If I can get out of here by six, that'll place me in Belton by midnight."

"Well, happy trails then," Penbrook said. He seemed disappointed and a little pissed off. Mackenzie assumed this was because he had been under the impression that she and Ellington were going to be by his side until the case was wrapped.

Making no real attempt to mask his feelings, Penbrook headed for the door. Barely looking over his shoulder at them, he gave a perfunctory wave. "Let us know if you need anything."

Once Penbrook had closed the door behind him, Mackenzie let out a sigh. "Wow," she said. "He really didn't take that very well, did he?"

Ellington took a moment to think of his response. When he did finally say something, his voice was low and measured. "I think I understand where he's coming from, though."

"How's that?" Mackenzie asked.

"The most recent deaths have all been around Omaha. To go all the way to the other end of the state seems like a needless errand."

"Everything started there," she said. "It just makes sense."

She could tell he wanted to get out of his seat and come to her—maybe to hug her or take her hands in his own. But he had worked hard on drawing the line between professionalism and their love life. Therefore, he remained in his seat.

"Look," he said. "I understand how much this case means to you. And I know you well enough to know that you won't stop until it's over. And if you want to head out to Belton, then I think you should. But…I think maybe I need to stay here."

She had never even considered going back to her hometown alone. She'd done it a little over a year ago but that had been different. Back then, she'd not had the support of Ellington to fall back on.

Apparently, her hurt and disappointment showed on her face because Ellington then *did* get out of his chair. He came to her and stepped directly in front of her. He took one of her hands, holding it lightly.

"I want to go. I do. But we've made this mistake before. We travel off somewhere that isn't central to the investigation only to realize when we come back that something monumental has happened. With this one, I don't think we can afford to do that. If you feel pulled out to Morrill County, then go. But I think I need to stay here at the field office. At the risk of coming off like a prick...this case isn't just about your dad. There are several dead bodies here in Omaha, too. Recent ones."

And of course he's right, she thought. *But at the same time...why abandon me when I need him the most?*

She nodded, though. She wasn't going to go all drama queen on him right now. Or ever, if she could help it. Besides...why should she be angry at him for successfully separating their professional relationship from their emotional one? She certainly wasn't doing a very good job of it at the moment.

"That makes sense," she said. "Maybe you can start canvassing the streets and talking to other vagrants."

"I was thinking the same thing. But look, Mac...if you want me with you..."

"No," she said. "I'm good. You're right. Let's do it your way."

She hated the fact that her disappointment was coming out. She knew he didn't doubt her instincts and she also knew that his approach of splitting up would be the most beneficial to the case. But she was headed back to her hometown to face demons she had only ignored and never truly put behind her. This was his first real chance to step up and show her the kind of man he could be for her.

But he was opting to be a better agent than a better boyfriend.

She understood it and, God help her, it made her fall for him a bit harder.

"I'm not stupid, Mac," he said. "You're mad. I can come with you. It's not a big deal."

"I'm not mad...not at you. I just hate the way this case is making me feel like two different people. But you're right. You need to stay here."

She gave him a small kiss on the corner of his mouth and headed for the door.

"You're leaving just like that?"

17

"It's better than prolonging it and getting even more upset, isn't it? I'll call you when I get a room."

"You're sure this is what you want?" he asked.

I don't know what I want, she thought. *And that's the problem.* Instead, she only said: "Yes. It's the smartest move and for the best. I'll talk to you around midnight."

With that, she left the conference room. It took everything in her not to turn around and explain to him that she had no idea why his suggestion of splitting up was bothering her so much. But instead, she forged on. She kept her eyes to the floor, not wanting to speak to anyone, as she headed to the AR desk to grab a car.

CHAPTER FIVE

In hindsight, Mackenzie wished she would have stayed in Omaha overnight and come into Morrill County in the light of day. Crossing into the small town of Belton at 12:05 at night was beyond creepy. There were hardly any other cars on the road and the only lights to be seen were the streetlights along Main Street and a few neon signs in the windows of bars and the one place she was actually looking for, the town's one motel.

Belton had a population of just over two thousand. It consisted mostly of farmers and textile plant workers. Small businesses were the heart of the place because no larger businesses dared try their hand in this part of the state. When she was a kid, a McDonald's, an Arby's, and a Wendy's had all tried to make a go of it along Main Street, but each of them had died out within three years.

She checked into a room after getting a not-so-subtle leering stare from the crusty old desk clerk. With her one single bag unpacked and the day having worn her down, she called Ellington before cutting the lights out. Ever dutiful, he answered on the second ring. He sounded about as tired as she felt.

"I made it," she said, not bothering with hello.

"Good," Ellington responded. "How are you?"

"Creeped out. It's a weird place to revisit after dark, I guess."

"You still think this was the right way to handle it?"

"Yeah. You?"

"I don't know. I've had some time to think about it. Maybe I should have come with you. It's more than just the case for you. You're trying to also put some of your past behind you. And if I love you, which I do, I should be there for that."

"But it's a case first," she said. "You have to be a good agent first."

"Yeah. I'll keep telling myself that. You sound beat, Mac. Get some sleep. That is, if you can sleep alone anymore."

She grinned. It had been nearly three months since they'd started sharing a bed on a regular basis. "Speak for yourself," she said. "I just got eye-humped by a particularly elderly desk clerk."

"Use protection," Ellington said with a chuckle. "Good night."

Mackenzie hung up and stripped down to her underwear. She slept above the covers, refusing to take the gamble of pulling back the sheets of a motel in Belton. She thought it would take forever for her to fall asleep, but before the solitude and quiet of the town outside the window had enough time to properly chill her, sleep snared her and pulled her down.

***

Her internal alarm woke her up at 5:45 but she ignored it and closed her eyes again. She had no real agenda pushing her and besides that, she couldn't remember the last time she'd allowed herself to sleep in. She managed to fall back to sleep and when she woke up again, it was 7:28. She rolled out of bed, showered, and got dressed. She was out the door by eight and instantly in search of coffee.

She grabbed a cup along with a sausage biscuit at a small diner that had been standing for as long as she could remember. She'd frequented it with her friends in high school, slurping milkshakes until the place closed down at nine every night. Now the place seemed like a greasy dump, a smear on how she remembered her teen years.

But the coffee was good and dark, the proper sort of fuel to push her down Highway 6 toward a plot of land where she had once lived. As she neared it, she found that she could easily recall the last time she had been out here. She had come in the company of Kirk Peterson, the now-troubled private investigator who had stumbled upon her father's case when Jimmy Scotts had been killed.

So when the house crept into view when she turned down the driveway, she wasn't all that surprised at what she saw. A deteriorating roof looked to be threatening to bring the entire rear wall down. The weeds around the place were rampant and the front porch looked like something out of a horror movie.

The neighbors' house was vacant too. It seemed fitting that there was nothing to either side of the houses but forest. Maybe one day the forest would creep in and swallow the old neglected houses up.

Wouldn't bother me at all, Mackenzie thought.

She parked her car in the ghost of a driveway and stepped out into the morning. With the highway behind her and the woods ahead, the place was still and serene. She could hear birdsong in the trees and the ticking of her car's engine as it cooled. She walked through the silence, right up to the front door. She smiled when she saw that it had been kicked in. She remembered doing it when she

20

had been out here with Peterson. She could also remember the sick sort of satisfaction she had derived from the act.

Inside, it was just as she had seen it a little over a year ago. No furniture, no belongings, not much of anything. Cracks in the walls, mold on the carpet, the smell of age and neglect. There was nothing here for her. Nothing new.

So why the hell am I here?

She knew the answer. She knew it was because she knew it would be the last time she ever saw it. After this trip, she would never allow herself to be bothered by this damned house. Not in her memories, not in her dreams, and sure as hell not in her future.

She walked through the house slowly, taking in every room. The living room, where she and her sister, Stephanie, had watched *The Simpsons* and had gotten borderline obsessed with *The X-Files.* The kitchen, where her mother had rarely served up anything worthwhile other than a lasagna that she had found the recipe for on a box of pasta. Her bedroom, where she had kissed a boy for the first time and had let a boy undress her for the first time. There were squares on her wall slightly discolored from the rest of the paint; this had been where her posters of Nine Inch Nails, Nirvana, and PJ Harvey had once hung.

The bathroom, where she'd cried a bit after getting her first period. The tiny laundry room, where she'd tried getting the smell of spilled beer from her blouse when she'd come in late one night at the age of fifteen.

Then at the end of the hall was her parents' room—the room that had haunted her dreams for far too long. The door was open, the room waiting for her. She didn't even enter the room, though. She stood at the doorway, her arms folded across her chest as she looked in. With morning sun coming in through the cracked and dusty windows, the room had an ethereal quality to it. It was easy to imagine the place as haunted or cursed. But she knew neither was true. A man had died in this room, his blood still on the carpet. But the same was true of countless other rooms in the world. This one was no more special than those other rooms. So why should it hold so much weight over her?

You can think you're tough and stubborn if you want, some wiser part of her spoke up. *But if you don't solve this case this time around, this room will always haunt you. You may as well clamp yourself to the floor and throw a prison gate up.*

She left that doorway and went outside. She walked around to the back of the house, where the only entry to the cellar was. She found the old door crooked in its frame and easy to open. She stepped inside and nearly screamed at the sight of a green snake slithering into one of the corners. She chuckled at herself and stepped into the dusty space. It reeked of old earth and weird sour things. It was a forgotten place with cobwebs and dust gathered everywhere. Dirt, dust, mildew, rot. It was hard to imagine this was where she had once been excited to venture into when it was time to pull her bike out in the spring and ride it around the yard. It had been where her father had kept the lawn mower and weed eater, where her mother had kept all of the empty Mason jars for making her jams and jellies.

Overcome with the memories and the rancid smell, Mackenzie stepped back outside. She headed for her car but was unable to leave just yet. Like a bored ghost, she once again went inside to haunt the space. She walked to the end of the hall, back to her parents' room.

She stared into the room, slowly starting to understand the route she needed to take. She'd been closer to it last night, driving into Belton and just wanting the ride to be over. This empty old room held nothing for her other than gruesome memories. If she wanted real progress on the case, she was going to have to do some digging.

She was going to have to hit the streets of the town that, as a teenager, she had feared she might never escape.

***

She'd been so removed from Belton once she had managed to land a job on the State Police as a twenty-three-year-old that the years had stripped knowledge from her. She had no idea which businesses would still be open. She also had no idea who had died and who had managed to live to a ripe old age.

Sure, she was less than a dozen years removed from living in Belton, but a single year had a funny way of causing chaos on a small town—be it finances, real estate, or deaths. But she also knew that small towns tended to keep their roots in tradition. And that's why Mackenzie drove to the local farm supply store at the far eastern end of town.

The place was called Atkins Farm and Tractor Supply and at one time, long before Mackenzie had been born, it had been the center of business in town. That's one of the stories her father had told her anyway. Now, though, it was a ghost of its former self. When Mackenzie had been a kid, the place had offered just about any sort of crop a farmer could want (specializing in corn like most places in Nebraska). It had also sold small farming equipment, accessories, and household goods.

When she walked into it fifteen minutes after standing in the doorway of the room her father had died in, Mackenzie almost felt sad for the owners. The entire back of the store, which had once held the crops and gardening supplies, had been gutted. There was now an old scratched up pool table sitting back there. In terms of the store itself, it still offered crops, but the selection was not much to speak of. The largest section of the place, in fact, was a display of flower and plant seeds. A small cooler in the back held fishing bait (minnows and night crawlers, according to the hand-drawn sign) while the front counter stood in front of a very dusty display of fishing rods and tackle boxes.

Two old men stood behind the counter. One was stirring a cup of coffee while the other one flipped through a supply book. She approached the counter, not quite sure which approach to take: the local returning after a long absence or an FBI agent digging up facts on an old case.

She figured she'd play it by ear. Both men looked to her at the same time, when she was just a few steps from the counter. She recognized both men from the years she had lived in Belton but only knew the name of the man flipping through the catalogue.

"Mr. Atkins?" she asked, knowing right away that she might be able to play both roles and get some honest information—if there was any to be had.

The man with the catalogue in his hands looked up at her. Wendell Atkins was twelve years older than the last time Mackenzie had seen him but he looked as if he had aged at least twenty. Mackenzie assumed he had to be at least seventy years old by now.

He smiled at her and cocked his head to the side. "You look familiar, but I don't know if the name is going to come to me," he said. "Might as well tell it to me because I could stand here and guess all day."

"I'm Mackenzie White. I lived in Belton for all of my life up until I was eighteen."

"White...your mom was Patricia?"

"Yes, sir. That's me."

"Well goodness," Atkins said. "I haven't seen you in a long time. Last I heard you were working for the State Police or something, right?"

"I was detective out there for a while," she said. "But I ended up in Washington, DC. I work for the FBI now."

She smiled internally because she knew that within an hour of her leaving here, Wendell Atkins would tell everyone he knew about his visit with Mackenzie White, the girl who went off to DC and became a fed. And if word got spread around, she figured some people might start to discuss what happened to her father. In small towns, that's how information was typically passed around.

"Is that so?" Atkins said. Even his friend now looked up from his coffee cup, looking very interested.

"Yes, sir. And that's actually why I'm here. I had to come out to Belton to look into an old case. My father's case, actually."

"Oh no," Atkins said. "That's right...they never did find who did that to him, did they?"

"They did not. And lately, there have been some murders out in Omaha that we think are linked to my father. Now, I'm coming here because, quite frankly, I remember Dad coming in here every now and then when I was a kid. It was the kind of place where men sort of just sat around drinking coffee and shooting the breeze, right?"

"That's right...though it wasn't always coffee we were drinking," Wendell said with a raspy little chuckle.

"I was wondering if you could tell me anything you remember hearing after my dad was killed. Even if you think it was just rumors or gossip, I'd like to know."

"Well, *Agent White*," he said with good humor, "I hate to say that some of it isn't too pleasant."

"I don't expect it to be."

Atkins made an uncomfortable sound in his throat as he leaned in slightly across the counter. His friend seemed to sense an awkward conversation on the way; he took his cup of coffee and disappeared behind the rows of inventory and fishing gear behind the counter.

"Some say it was your mother," Atkins said. "And I'm only telling you this because you asked. Otherwise, I wouldn't dare comment on such a thing."

"It's okay, Mr. Atkins."

"The story goes that she set it up to look like a murder. The fact that she...well, that she sort of had that breakdown afterwards seemed a little too convenient to some folks."

Mackenzie couldn't even be upset at the accusation. She'd pondered this theory herself, but it just didn't check out. It would mean she was also responsible for the deaths of the vagrants, Gabriel Hambry, and Jimmy Scotts. Her mother was many things, but she was not a serial killer.

"Another story says that your father was tied up with some bad folks from Mexico. A drug cartel of some kind. A deal went bad or your dad stiffed them somehow and that was the end of it."

This was another theory that had long been speculated. The fact that Jimmy Scotts had also allegedly been involved with a drug cartel—his in New Mexico—provided a link, but, as a lengthy investigation had proven, there was no connection. Then again, Mackenzie's father had been on the force and it was public knowledge that he had taken down a few local drug dealers, so the assumption was an easy one to make.

"Anything else?" she asked.

"No. Believe what you want, but I honestly don't pry too much. I hate gossip. I wish I had more to tell you."

"It's okay. Thanks, Mr. Atkins."

"You know," he said, "you might want to talk to Amy Lucas. Do you remember her?"

Mackenzie tried to jog her memory but nothing came to mind. "The name rings a very small bell, but no…I don't remember her."

"She lives out on Dublin Road…the white house with the old Cadillac up on blocks in the driveway. The damn thing has been there forever."

Sadly enough, that was all the reminder Mackenzie needed. While she did not personally know Amy Lucas, she *did* remember the house. The Cadillac in question was from the '60s. It had been up on blocks for God only knew how long. Mackenzie could remember seeing it from her time in Belton.

"What about her?" Mackenzie asked.

"Her and your mother were as thick as thieves at one point. Amy lost her husband to cancer three years ago. She hasn't really been a fixture in town like she used to be since then. But I remember her and your mother, always hanging out together. They were always out at the bar, or playing cards on Amy's front porch."

As if Mr. Atkins had hit a switch somewhere, Mackenzie suddenly remembered more than she had before. She could just barely see Amy Lucas's face, highlighted by a cigarette poking out from between her lips. *She's the friend Mom and Dad got into so many arguments about,* Mackenzie thought. *On the nights Mom came home drunk or just wasn't around on a Saturday, she was with Amy. I was too young to even think twice about any of it.*

"Do you know where she works?" Mackenzie asked.

"Nowhere. I bet you anything she's in her house right now. When her husband died, she got left with a nice little nest egg. She just sits in her house and mopes all day. But please…if you go see

25

her, for the love of all that's holy, don't let her know I sent you that way."

"I won't. Thanks again, Mr. Atkins."

"Sure. I hope you find whatever it is you're looking for."

"Me, too."

She stepped back outside and walked to her car. She looked up and down the quiet stretch of Main Street and started to wonder: *What, exactly, am I looking for?*

She got into her car and started for Dublin Road, hoping she'd find some semblance of an answer there.

CHAPTER SIX

Dublin Road was a two-lane stretch of blacktop that wound through the forest. Towering trees to both sides of the road escorted Mackenzie to Amy Lucas's residence. She felt like she was being transported through time, especially when she came to the house and saw that old Cadillac, sitting up on blocks at the far end of the gravel driveway.

She parked behind the only other car in the driveway, a much more current Honda, and got out. As she stepped up onto the porch, she thought of Mr. Atkins telling her about her mother and Amy playing cards in this very space. The knowledge of her mother having at one time occupied the porch sent a small shiver through her.

Mackenzie knocked on the door and it was answered right away. The woman who stood on the other side was a ghost of the memory Mackenzie had. Amy Lucas appeared to be in her early fifties and had the sort of eyes that always seemed to be suspicious of someone. Most of her brown hair had already gone gray. It was pulled back tight to reveal a forehead pocked with old acne scars. She had a cigarette between the fingers of her right hand, the smoke drifting back into the house.

"Mrs. Lucas?" Mackenzie asked. "Amy Lucas?"

"That's me," she said. "Who are you?"

Mackenzie flashed her badge and went through the same old routine. "Mackenzie White, with the FBI. I was hoping to ask—"

"Mac! Holy shit! What are you doing in town?"

The fact that this woman apparently remembered her well threw Mackenzie off a bit but she managed to keep her composure. "I'm actually working on a case and I was hoping you could be of some help."

"Me?" She then laughed the kind of laugh that had long ago become the sound of countless cigarettes working against her lungs.

"Well, it's about my dad's case. And quite frankly, Mom and I aren't on the best terms anymore. I was hoping you could maybe help shed some light on a few things."

Those suspicious eyes narrowed for a moment before Amy nodded her head and stepped aside. "Come on in," she said.

Mackenzie stepped inside and was smacked in the face by the stench of cigarette smoke. It was almost like a visible cloud hanging in the house. Amy led her through a small foyer and into the living room, where she took a seat in an old tattered armchair.

As Mackenzie sat down on the edge of a couch on the far wall, she did her best to cover up the fact that she was trying not to cough from all the cigarette smoke.

"I heard about your husband," Mackenzie said. "My condolences."

"Yeah, it was a sad day, but we knew it was coming. Cancer can be a bitch. But...he was ready to go. The pain was so bad there near the end."

There was no easy transition and, since Mackenzie had never considered the art of conversation her strong point, she did her best to get to the point without seeming rude.

"So, I've come back into town to try to find more details on my father's murder. The case was cold for the longest time but another series of murders elsewhere in the state have us looking back into it. I wanted to come to you because you seem to have been close with my mother. I was wondering if there's anything you can tell me about the state she might have been in during the days just before and just after my father's death."

Amy took a drag from her cigarette and sat back in her chair. She no longer looked suspicious, but now quite sad.

"Damn, I miss your mother. How is she?"

"I don't know," Mackenzie said. "We haven't spoken in over a year. There are some unresolved issues there, as you might imagine."

Amy nodded. "Did she ever make it out of that...home?"

She means the psych ward, Mackenzie thought. "Yes. And then she got an apartment somewhere and lived her own life. She sort of left Stephanie and I behind."

"When your father died, it was so hard on her," Amy said. "The fact that she was right there, on the couch, when it happened—it messed her up."

Yeah, it fucked me up pretty bad, too, Mackenzie thought. "Yeah, we were all there. Did Mom ever say anything to you about that night? Maybe things she saw or heard?"

"Not that I can remember. I do know that she was haunted by the idea that the door must have been unlocked—that the person that came in and killed your father just walked right into the house. It freaked her out that it could have been you or your sister."

"And that's just it," Mackenzie said. "Everyone else was left safe and sound. The killer only wanted my father. Did Mom ever share things with you about my father that you thought were strange? Maybe reasons someone might want him dead?"

"Honestly, your mom only ever talked about how hot he was in that police uniform. He was a detective near the end, though, right?"

"Right. So…did Mom like the fact that he was a cop or did that make her uneasy?"

"A bit of both, I think. She was very proud of him but she was always worried. It's why she drank so much. She was always worried he was going to get hurt and the drinking was her way of handling the stress."

"I see…"

"Look, I know some of the gossip around town may not be so nice, but your mother did love your father. She loved him very much. He went out of his way to support her. When he first became a cop and they could barely meet the bills, he even got a loan and bought this tiny little apartment building outside of town. He tried to be a landlord for about two years and it just wasn't for him. The income was enough to keep them afloat, though."

"When was this?" she asked.

"Before you came along, for sure," Amy said. "We were all so young back then. God, I can't believe I forget about some of it so easily…"

Mackenzie couldn't help but smile. Just like that, she'd learned something new about her father. Sure, maybe he and his mother had mentioned his little landlord endeavor in passing but if they had, she had never picked up on it.

"Amy, when was the last time you spoke with my mother?"

"The day before she left to go off to that home. Not to rub it in, but even then I think she was upset with you. But she never gave any good reason why."

"And did she say anything about my father?"

"She said it happened like a nightmare. She said it was her fault and she should have been able to stop it. I figured it was just guilt from having been asleep and not waking up when someone apparently came into the house with a gun."

"Anything else you can think of?" Mackenzie asked.

Even as Amy gave this some thought, Mackenzie had latched on to one thing Amy had said. *She should have been able to stop it.*

Seems like a strange thing to say in light of what happened.

She knows something. She always has and I've been too damned scared to ask...

Shit. I have to call her.

Amy finally answered with: "No, nothing that I can remember. But you've jogged my memory on the past now. If I think of anything else, I'll certainly let you know."

"I'd appreciate that," Mackenzie said, handing Amy one of her business cards.

She left the house, blessedly glad to be able to breathe in the fresh air. She headed back to her car, aware the she reeked of cigarette smoke, but still pondering the new bit of information she'd learned about her father.

A landlord, she thought. *I can't see that at all! I wonder if Stephanie knew...*

But on the heels of that was another thought.

I'm going to have to visit my mother. I can't get around it any longer.

This knowledge made her instantly nervous. As she pulled back out onto Dublin Road, the mere thought of seeing her mother set her on edge. It felt like a weight was settling in her stomach as she headed back into town, trying to think of anything she could do to put off the inevitable visit with her mother.

CHAPTER SEVEN

She did have one more legitimate task to carry out before she tormented herself with further thoughts of her mother. She looked into the case files and pulled up the information on her father's autopsy. She found the name of the coroner who had written the original report and set about finding him.

It was fairly easy. While the coroner in question had retired two years ago, Morrill County was the type of place that felt like a black hole. It was impossible to escape it. That's why there were so many familiar faces she saw on the streets. No one had thought to leave, to go elsewhere into the world to see what life had for them.

She'd placed a call to Agent Harrison back in DC to get the address of Jack Waggoner, the coroner who had worked on her father. She had the address within just a few minutes and found herself driving to another small town called Denbrough. Denbrough sat forty miles south of Belton, two little blips on the map that was Morrill County.

Jack Waggoner lived in a house that sat next door to a large meadow. Old ruined fence posts and barbed wire indicated there had once been horses or cattle there. When she parked her car in the driveway of a beautiful two-story Colonial-style house, she saw a woman pulling weeds out of a flower garden that traced the entire porch.

The woman eyed her from the moment Mackenzie turned the car in until she had parked it and got out.

"Hello," Mackenzie said, wanting to interact with the woman as soon as possible before the staring started to irritate her.

"Hey yourself," the woman said. "Who might you be?"

Mackenzie took out her badge and introduced herself as pleasantly as she could. Right away, the woman's eyes lit up, and she no longer looked at her suspiciously.

"And what brings the FBI out to Denbrough?" the woman asked.

"I was hoping to speak with Mr. Waggoner," she said. "Jack Waggoner. Is he home?"

"He is," the woman said. "I'm Bernice, by the way. His wife of thirty-one years. He gets calls from the government sometimes, always about dead folks he's seen in the past."

31

"Yeah, that's why I've come by. Could you get him for me?"

"I'll take *you* to *him*," Bernice said. "He's in the middle of a project."

Bernice led Mackenzie into the house. It was clean and sparsely decorated, making it seem much larger than it actually was. The makeup of the place again made her think that the huge field outside had once held cattle—cattle that had helped pay for such a house.

Bernice led her down into a finished basement. When they came to the bottom of the stairs, the first thing Mackenzie saw was a deer head on the wall. Then, as they turned the corner, she saw a small stuffed dog—a real dog that had been stuffed after death. It was perched in the corner on a strange sort of platform.

In the far corner of the basement, a man sat hunched over a worktable. A desk lamp was shining on something that he was working on, the something hidden by the man's hunched back and shoulders.

"Jack?" Bernice said. "You've got a visitor."

Jack Waggoner turned around and took in Mackenzie with a pair of thick glasses on. He removed them, blinked his eyes almost comically, and slowly got out of his chair. When he moved, Mackenzie could see what he was working on. She saw the body of what looked to be a small bobcat.

Taxidermy, she thought. *He just couldn't get away from dead bodies after retirement, it seems.*

"I don't believe we've met," Jack said.

"We haven't," she said. "I'm Mackenzie White with the FBI. I was hoping to speak with you about a body you profiled and assisted with about seventeen years ago."

Jack whistled and shrugged. "Hell, I can barely remember the bodies I saw during my last year—and that was just two years ago. Seventeen years might be pushing it."

"It was a pretty high-profile case," she said. A policeman...a detective, actually. A man named Benjamin White. He was my father. He was shot point—"

"Point-blank in the back of the head," Jack said. "With a Beretta 92, if memory serves correct."

"It does."

"Yeah, that one I do remember. And...well, I suppose it's nice to meet you. Sorry about your father, of course."

Bernice sighed and started toward the stairs. She gave an apologetic little smile and wave to Mackenzie as she excused herself.

Jack smiled at his wife as she headed up the stairs. When her footfalls had faded, Jack looked back to the work table. "I'd shake your hand but…well, I don't know if you want to."

"Taxidermy seems like a fitting hobby for a man with your work history," Mackenzie said.

"It passes the time. And the supplemental income doesn't hurt, either. Anyway…I digress. What can I answer for you about Ben White's case?"

"Honestly, I'm just looking for anything out of the ordinary. I've read the case reports more than fifty times, I'm sure. I know it front and back. But I'm also well aware that there are often tiny details only noticed by one or two people—details that don't seem like they are worth including at the time—that don't go in the official report. I'm looking for things like that."

Jack took a moment to think about it but Mackenzie could tell by the disappointed look in his eyes that he wasn't coming up with anything. After a few moments, he shook his head. "Sorry. But in terms of the body itself, there was nothing out of the ordinary. Obviously, the means of death was clear. Other than that, though, his body had been in good shape."

"So then why do you remember it so well?"

"Because of the nature of the case itself. It always struck me as fishy as hell. Your father was a well-respected cop. Someone came into your house, shot him in the back of the head, and managed to get out without anyone seeing who did it. A Beretta 92 isn't incredibly loud, but it's loud enough to wake up a household."

"It woke me up," Mackenzie said. "My room was directly next to his. I heard it but wasn't sure what it was. Then I heard footsteps as someone walked by my room. My bedroom door was closed, something I never did as a kid. I always left a crack. But someone had closed it. The same someone, I assume, that shot my father."

"That's right. You found him, didn't you?"

She nodded. "And it couldn't have been any more than two or three minutes after the gunshot. It took me that long to figure out that something was wrong. That's when I got out of bed and went to my parents' room to check."

"I tell you…I wish I had more for you. And please forgive me for saying so, but something about the official story just doesn't add up. Have you spoken to your mother about any of it?"

"No. Not at length. We aren't exactly the best of friends."

"She was a wreck in the days leading up to the funeral. No one could say a word to her. She went from inconsolable weeping to fits of rage in the blink of an eye."

Mackenzie nodded but said nothing. She could intimately remember her mother's fits of rage. It was one of the key factors in having her admitted to a psych ward later on.

"Was there any sort of secrecy involved when the body arrived at the morgue?" she asked.

"Not that I can remember. No shady business as far as I know. It was just another routine body being delivered. But you know…I do remember one policeman that was always around. He was with them when the body was delivered and he stayed around the medical office for a while, like he was waiting on something. Pretty sure I spied him at the funeral, too. I mean, Benjamin White was a well-respected guy…especially by other officers on the force. But this officer…he was there *all of the time.* If memory serves correct, he sort of hung back at the funeral, like he needed time alone to process or something. But this was forever ago, mind you. Seventeen years is a long time. Memories sort of start to slip away when you get to be my age."

"Would you happen to know this cop's name?" she asked.

"I don't. But I'm pretty sure he signed some paperwork at some point. Maybe if you can get your hands on the original case files?"

"Maybe," Mackenzie said.

He's telling the truth and *he feels sorry for me,* Mackenzie thought. *Nothing else to be had here…except maybe learning some taxidermy skills.*

"Thank you for your time, Mr. Waggoner," she said.

"Of course," he said, escorting her back upstairs. "I truly do hope you can wrap this one up. I always thought there was something off about the case. And even though I didn't know your father all that well, I always heard nothing but good things."

"I appreciate that," Mackenzie said.

With a final thanks, Mackenzie headed back outside with Jack at her side. She gave a wave to Bernice, back to the weeds in the flower garden, and got into her car. It was three in the afternoon but she felt like it was much later. She guessed the flight from DC to Nebraska, followed almost right away by a six-hour drive, was catching up to her.

It was too early to call it a day, though. She figured she could end her day by visiting the one place she figured she'd always end up, yet had never stepped foot in before: the Belton police station.

CHAPTER EIGHT

The Belton police station reminded her far too much of the station she had spent so much time in during her time as an officer and detective in southern Nebraska before the bureau had come calling. It was smaller but seemed to have that same sort of suffocating feel to it. It was literally like taking one big step back into her past.

After being buzzed through into the main area by a woman at a check-in kiosk, Mackenzie walked to a small room in the back of the building. A placard by the side of the door read RECORDS. It was almost appalling how lackadaisical the process was. She had shown her badge to the woman at the front kiosk. She made a call, got clearance, and then buzzed her through.

And that was it. On her way to the records room, two officers walking the hallways nodded to her and gave her strange looks but that was it. No one stopped her and no one asked what she was up to. Honestly, that was fine with her. The fewer distractions, the quicker she could get out of there.

The records room consisted of a small oak table in the center of the room, bookended by two chairs. The rest of the room was wall-to-wall filing cabinets, some of which looked old and beaten up, others much newer. She was surprised at how organized the files were, the older cabinets holding files from as far back as 1951. For the sake of curiosity and her appreciation for well-maintained records and files, she pulled one of these drawers open and peeked inside. Well-worn pages, folders, and other materials rested neatly inside, though it was clear from the smell of old paper and the wafting of dust that they had not been viewed in a very long time.

She closed the drawer and then scanned the labels on the front of the other cabinets until she found the one she needed. She pulled the drawer open and started to sift through the files. The good thing about being a police officer in such a small town was that there usually weren't many cases worth recording. When she'd started doing the digging into her father's case, she discovered that on the year he'd died, there had only been two homicides in all of Belton.

Because of this, it was very easy for her to find her father's file. She pulled it out, frowning at how thin the folder was. She even

35

looked back into the drawer to see if there was another file that she had missed, but there was nothing else.

Resigned to the single thin folder, Mackenzie sat down at the little table in the center of the room and started to look through the folder. There were several photographs of the crime scene, all of which she had seen. She also read over the notes on the case. She'd seen these, too; she even had photocopies of them in her own collection of records on the case. But to see the original documents—to hold them in her hands—seemed to make it more real somehow.

There were a few documents in the file that she did not have personal copies of. Among them was a copy of the coroner's report, complete with Jack Waggoner's name signed at the bottom. She looked it over, found the work and notes satisfactory, and carried on to the next page. She wasn't sure what she was looking for, but there was nothing new to see. However, when she got to the back of the file, she came across page two of the final report, where a note maintained that the case was unresolved.

At the bottom, there were two scrawled signatures, along with each officer's printed name. One was Dan Smith. The other was Reggie Thompson.

Mackenzie flipped back to the coroner's report to see the names of the officers that had signed off there as well. There was only one name there: Reggie Thompson. Thompson's name on both of the documents was a good indicator that he was the officer who seemed to have been hovering over the case, even at the coroner's office.

She flipped through the files one more time to make sure she hadn't missed anything. As she had suspected, there was nothing. She put the file back in the cabinet and left the room. When she walked back out into the hallway, she took her time. She looked at the placards on the walls by the each doorway. Most of the doors were open, with no one occupying the desks inside. It wasn't until she got to the end of the hall, nearly back to the small bullpen area and the check-in kiosk beyond, that she found an occupied office.

She knocked on the partially open door and got a cheerful "Come in" in response.

Mackenzie stepped inside the office and was greeted by a plump woman sitting behind a desk. She was typing something into her computer, not coming to a stop even when she looked up at Mackenzie.

"Can I help you?" the lady asked.

"I'm looking for an Officer Reggie Thompson," Mackenzie said.

This seemed to get the woman's attention. She stopped typing and looked up at Mackenzie with a frown. Knowing what was coming, Mackenzie showed the lady her badge and gave her name.

"Oh, I see," the lady said. "In that case, I'm sorry to say that Officer Thompson retired last year. He hung in there as long as he could, but he had to stop eventually. He was diagnosed with prostate cancer. From what I hear, he's beating it but it's taken a toll on him."

"Do you know if he's up for visitors? I was hoping to ask him some questions about a case he was working a while back."

"I'm pretty sure he'd love that, actually. He calls here at least once a week just to catch up...to see what kind of cases he's missing. But if I were you, I'd wait until tomorrow. From what his wife tells me, he overdoes himself in the mornings and early afternoons, so he's wiped out by two or three in the afternoon."

"I'll wait until tomorrow, then," Mackenzie said. "Thanks for your help."

Mackenzie left the station with the same lack of activity she had experienced in coming in. All told, she'd spent about half an hour there and while she still had a small chunk of the afternoon at her disposal, she was feeling tired. And since Reggie Thompson preferred to do his business in the morning, that left her with no options.

She left the station and headed back for the motel. On the way, her phone rang and she was happy to see that it was Ellington. While they weren't *technically* in the midst of a fight, it was still strange to be at odds with him.

He's doing what's right, she told herself. *Give the man a break.*

She answered the call with a quick: "Hey. How's it going?"

"I've spoken to at least a dozen different vagrants today. I have a whole new appreciation for what they go through but I have also come to the conclusion that they are not the most reliable of sources. How about you?"

"Making progress," she said, though it felt like a lie. "I spoke to a few locals that gave me some insights into the case—small-town gossip really, but there are usually kernels of truth on those grapevines. Spoke to the coroner that handled Dad's body and then stopped by the local PD to check the files. Got the name of an officer who seemed to be attached to the case and I'm speaking with him tomorrow."

"You sure as hell got more done than I did," he said. "How much longer do you think you'll be there?"

"I don't know. It depends on what tomorrow brings—both here and in Omaha. What's the general mood down there?"

Ellington hesitated before answering. "If I'm being honest, it's tense. Penbrook is pissed that you so casually took a trip out west. He's being as helpful as he can be, but he's letting me know in no uncertain terms that he's not happy."

"And you?"

"The same as last night. I wish I was there with you...or that you were still here. But dividing and conquering was the best choice. I think even Penbrook realizes it. But if I'm being honest, the general consensus here in Omaha is that you're using this as a hometown tour to revisit the past."

"That consensus is stupid," she said. She hated that the comeback sounded so juvenile.

"You have to understand what it looks like," he argued. "You were here for less than a day and then hauled ass off to Morrill County, all by yourself. That's how they're seeing it anyway."

"This is not a hometown tour. I am not getting any sort of pleasure out of this."

"I know that. But Penbrook and his cronies don't know you as well as I do. They get that it's personal, but they don't understand it." He paused here and then added: "Don't bullshit me, Mac. How are you holding up?"

"I'm tired and I'm anxious and quite frankly, I wish some arsonist had burned my childhood home to the ground a long time ago."

"If you light the match, I won't tell anyone."

"Don't tempt me. I'll talk to you later."

She ended the call, let out a shaky sigh, and tossed her phone into the passenger seat. She drove through Belton, recalling what it had been like to be a typical angsty teenager, mad at her mother, her sister, the police for not finding her father's killer—the whole world, it seemed.

And while she had grown up significantly since then, there was a part of her that understood how a place like Belton could cause that sort of teenage angst to grow and fester. There were only churches, bars, and grocery stores. Oh, and trees, corn, and wide expanses of land that seemed to have no end.

Mackenzie was starting to feel that angst again as she pulled into the parking lot of the motel. And the sad thing was that she missed it. Whether it was the town, being so close to her father's case again, or a combination of both, Mackenzie felt herself growing angry for no particular reason and allowing herself to embrace it.

And that was fine. Because for the time being, it felt pretty damned good.

***

There were times when she lay down to sleep that she knew there would be a nightmare. It was almost like an alarm in her head, alerting her to the fact. She knew she'd have one that night but was drifting off before she had time to really even worry about it.

This one started in a surreal way; it made her feel like she was watching a 3D movie with a grainy set of glasses. She was watching it all through someone else's eyes, like an art-house point-of-view film.

He takes the first step up onto the small porch and, as expected, finds the door unlocked. He hesitates before opening it, savoring the peaceful night all around him. He then places his hand on the doorknob and turns it. It opens easily enough and he walks into the home of Ben and Patricia White.

Patricia White is asleep on the couch. There's a bottle of red wine on the floor, along with an empty wine glass. The television is on but the volume is muted so low that he can barely hear the dialogue from the news program. He looks at the sleeping woman and thinks about the things he could do to her. He could kill her, too. Or do what he came here to do and then come back and rape her. It wasn't in the plan, but there was always time for a little unscripted fun.

He passes the couch and leaves the living room. He passes through the kitchen without a single look around. The shapes of the fridge and the small kitchen table are murky in the weak light. He then makes his way down the hallway. He opens the first door and sees a girl of about six or seven. Very small, very cute. Stephanie White. She's sleeping with her back to him.

He studies the little girl for just a moment before leaving her be, closing the door quietly behind him. He then tries the next room and sees another little girl. This one is older...maybe ten or so. She's sleeping on her back, her mouth a little agape as tiny snores escape. He studies her the same way he studied the other girl, only taking more time to appreciate the curves that were almost appearing on her body.

He leaves her alone, again quietly closing the door behind him. The next door along the hallway is the bathroom. It's in disarray, a crumpled towel on the floor and someone's dirty clothes from the day thrown at the hamper but not making it in.

He leaves the bathroom, checks back down the hall to make sure he hasn't stirred the wife or the daughters, and then enters the bedroom.

Benjamin White is lying there, just like he's supposed to. The other side of the bed is empty, his wife passed out on the couch.

He approaches the bed and pulls the gun from his pocket. It's a Beretta 92, fairly light and somewhat common. He cocks it as if he has done it a thousand times before. The next three seconds are fluid and effortless.

He places the gun to the back of Benjamin White's head at an upward tilt and pulls the trigger. The blast is not muffled but still surprisingly quiet.

Blood splatters everywhere as Benjamin White's body jerks a single time. Blood on the walls, on the sheets, on the carpet, on his shirt, blood everywhere and—

Mackenzie woke up with a gasp.

She'd seen it through the killer's eyes. That was certainly new. She'd dreamed about the room and that particular scene hundreds of times but had never seen it like that. It made her feel a little sick to her stomach.

She looked at the clock and saw that it was 4:56. She'd slept for about seven hours—plenty of sleep as far as she was concerned. Not bothering to try for another hour or so, she rolled out of bed. While in the shower, she focused on the scene from her dream where the killer had looked in on her. It had been surreal and even now, she felt like there was someone standing on the other side of the shower curtain, watching her.

Of course, when she was out of the shower, there was no one there. She dried off and got dressed, checking her phone for any messages she might have missed while in the shower. There was nothing at all.

She looked herself over in the mirror, deciding to hit up the same diner from yesterday for breakfast. After that, she'd visit Reggie Thompson, whom she had discovered via a phone request through Harrison lived right there in Belton.

The possibility of visiting her mother was still there, too. It would simply not leave her head and continued to rattle around like an empty aluminum can.

Maybe later, she thought. It had always been her internal response to any thought of reaching out to her mother. *Maybe later.*

She left the motel room and stepped out into the early morning. All was quiet, all was still. And she found that with that familiar angst she'd experienced yesterday came another familiar feeling from her teenage years: to get the hell out of Belton as soon as she could.

CHAPTER NINE

Reggie Thompson lived in a modest house tucked away on one of the secondary roads behind Main Street. It was a quaint house, surrounded by a well-maintained lawn with numerous towering trees. As Mackenzie walked up to his doorstep, she watched as two squirrels ran precariously along the branches of one tree while making their way to the next.

She knocked on the door, instantly feeling like an intruder. The poor man was suffering from cancer. She'd like to think that if the woman at the station yesterday had not told her that he would love to have her visit, she would have stayed away because of his situation. But she knew that wasn't true. Not only was he a reliable source of information she was looking for, but the case was slowly getting her obsessed.

The door was answered by a woman who looked to be in her early sixties. She carried a cup of tea in one hand, the smell of which perked Mackenzie up. She eyed Mackenzie curiously and said simply: "Hello?"

"Hi," Mackenzie said, going through her routine. She showed the lady her badge and gave her name. "I'm looking for Reggie Thompson. I understand he's been through a hard time lately, but someone I spoke with at the police station yesterday seemed to think he'd appreciate the visit."

"Is it about a case?" the woman asked.

"It is…about an older case from nearly twenty years ago."

"In that case, let's get you inside. I'm Mary, by the way. I'm the one that has to hear his old stories and listen to him grumble about how much he misses it. Did they tell you that he calls the station at least once a week to get details on new cases?"

"It might have been mentioned," Mackenzie said as she was welcomed into the house.

Mary led Mackenzie to the back of the house, taking her through a small but gorgeous kitchen and a small mudroom. Off of the mudroom, there was a sun porch. Reggie Thompson was sitting in a rocking chair, reading a book as the morning sun filled the space. He looked up as the two women came out onto the porch. He smiled, but had a curious look about him.

42

"You have a visitor," Mary said with a mocking tone, as if she was playing the part of a secretary.

"Mackenzie White, FBI," Mackenzie said. She stepped to him and offered her hand so he would not be tempted to stand.

"I didn't do anything too bad these last few weeks," he joked. "Although on some of those meds I take, there's no telling what I'm apt to do."

"Enjoy," Mary said sarcastically as she slowly stepped back into the house.

"I'm sorry to stop by uninvited," Mackenzie said, taking a seat in a second rocking chair directly beside Reggie's. She assumed it was Mary's, the two of them sitting out here for the morning and afternoon sunlight.

"Mr. Thompson, I'm in town to try to wrap up a case that seems to span over nearly twenty years. And it started right here in Belton, seventeen years ago, when Benjamin White was killed. I saw your name on some of the case files and was hoping you could give me some perspective."

"Fortunately, that's an easy case to remember," Reggie said. "I did my best to stay as close to it as I could because something just didn't add up, as far as I was concerned."

"The coroner said there was an officer that was always there, every step of the way. That he even hung around for a while after the funeral. Was that you, by any chance?"

"It was. And I'm sorry...but I'm just putting two and two together here. You said your name was Mackenzie White, right?"

"I did."

"Was Ben your father?"

"He was."

"My God. I'm so sorry. But...I suppose it's some sort of cosmic justice that you ended up working the case. Can I ask why you're back out here all these years later?"

She hesitated a moment and then filled him in on the details of the case. She told him about Gabriel Hambry and Jimmy Scotts without giving names. She then told him about the vagrants and the business cards.

"I remember the business card," he said. "Did they have end up finding a business with that name?"

"One. Somewhere in New York. But it closed down in the late seventies and all of the follow-ups checked out. There's no connection there. So, you say you feel that things just didn't add up with the case. Can you give me some examples?"

"Well, your mother for one....forgive me for saying so. But how did the killer come in, pull off a shot, and then escape without your mother knowing or seeing anything? It seems odd to me. I'm not saying there was collusion or anything like that, but...it's damned weird."

"Anything else?"

"Well, you have to think—at the time, your father was a respected detective and pretty much everyone on the force looked up to him. He was a fine man, Agent White. And everyone on the force put in time trying to find his killer. But after about four months and nothing but dead ends, the orders came from higher up the ladder that we give it a rest. And they were *adamant* about it."

"Who gave the orders?"

"Our chief. In fact, it was one of the first things I decided to start digging into when I retired. But I found nothing. It was made even harder by the fact that the two men that were in charge of basically having us stop searching are both dead. The chief died of a heart attack about ten years ago and his superior was killed by a drunk driver three Christmases ago."

"Do you suspect some sort of foul play from within the department?"

"Not really. Not directly, anyway. But...there were always rumors among the department that your father had taken on some sort of undercover assignment to crack a drug ring. You hear about that?"

"Yeah. No one ever confirmed it, though."

"That's right. But the fact that some higher-ups wanted the case closed before it was solved makes that rumor seem to have some feet. Because another rumor going around was that there were some guys in the department that were taking money to assist local deals associated with that ring."

"The fact that you keep saying *rumor* makes me think there's nothing solid to it."

Reggie smiled at her and said, "So you can see why the case always got on my nerves. It's like opening this promising puzzle and then putting it all together only to find there are about a dozen or so pieces missing."

"Did you ever speak to my mother during the case?" Mackenzie asked.

"I did. She was pretty much catatonic the first time, though. After that, she was like a zombie. Always staring off into space. It was hard to talk to her because she felt like it was her fault. The guilt was killing her."

44

"And she never said anything suspicious?"

"No. Other than trying to blame herself. She said it was the wine. She'd had too much to drink and passed out. That's why she neglected to lock the door and didn't stir awake when someone came into the house, fired the shot, and then left."

"But still…who would know the door was unlocked? Or did the killer come, ready to break in, and it was just a happy coincidence that the door happened to be unlocked?"

"That's one of the many questions I asked myself over and over again."

"What were some others?"

He looked off into his backyard, where a cat was sunning itself by the steps of the porch. He frowned and asked: "Can I be blunt?"

"Of course."

"Your mother never once asked if we had caught the guy or even if we were close. Even for people wrapped up in guilt, in my experience they are still very interested in the status of the case. But she never asked a single time. For the longest time, I just assumed that she didn't care about getting justice."

This sank in slowly and Mackenzie's mind flashed to the imagery of that night that her brain had long ago created. She had, of course, not seen her mother on the couch until after she had seen her dead father. But she had always imagined her passed out on the couch, bottle of wine and empty glass on the floor in front of her, useless and unaware. She saw that image again in that moment and it made her angry.

"Have you looked through the old files down at the station?" Reggie asked.

"I have. And I've had copies of them for years."

Reggie smiled. "I take it you're the obsessive type? If so, you got it naturally. Whenever your father latched on to a case, that was the end of it. It's all his mind focused on."

Mackenzie smiled even though she remembered many fights between her mother and father about how he always took his job too seriously—often choosing it over his wife.

"Thank you for speaking with me," Mackenzie said, getting to her feet.

"No problem. It's the most interesting thing that has happened to me in weeks. I take it you have easy access to my number if you have any other questions?"

"Yes, sir. And I may take you up on that."

Reggie nodded. "Agent White…I won't lie. I didn't know your father very well. We were on a first-name basis and I spoke to him maybe once a week, but only niceties. But based on what I know of him, I can safely say he'd be proud of you."

The sting of tears came out of nowhere and she could feel her cheeks turning red. She blinked furiously, trying to fend them off.

"Thanks," she mumbled and took her leave from the sun porch. Even when she passed through the Thompsons' kitchen and Mary said goodbye, Mackenzie never looked up from the floor as she did her best to escape the house before she had some sort of breakdown. Yet by the time she made it out to the front porch, she was openly crying and that, like the thought of her stupid useless mother passed out on the couch, pissed her off, too.

CHAPTER TEN

She had her mother's address on a folded Post-it note in her wallet. She'd tucked it away there two years ago, knowing that at some point in her life, she'd have to speak to the woman. She had known from as early as the age of eighteen that their paths would have to cross again. And based on the few awkward conversations they'd had over the last ten years, it was obvious that any meeting would not be a pleasant one.

Still, Mackenzie found herself sitting in the parking lot of the motel she had been staying in, looking at that Post-it note. Boone's Mill, Nebraska. She'd gotten out of Morrill County, not returning after she had come out of the psychiatric home. She'd been living in Boone's Mill for eight years, a little over two hours from where Mackenzie currently sat. So while she *had* gotten away, she hadn't ventured out very far.

Weird, Mackenzie thought. *If I was trying to get away from a past like hers, I'd move as far away as possible.*

But the fact of the matter was that she had no idea what her mother was up to these days. Was she working? Was she on welfare, sitting at home drinking herself away to daytime TV? Or was she dead? Mackenzie hadn't spoken to her in nearly a year and that one last conversation lasted less than three minutes.

One way to find out, she thought, slowly typing the address into her GPS app. *And let's not even try to pretend you aren't going. It's the next logical step in the process.*

Mackenzie pressed ENTER once the address was typed in.

"Fuck," she said.

She took a deep breath, pulled out of the parking lot, and headed north, toward her mother.

***

She arrived at the address in Boone's Mill at 11:20. After knocking on the front door, she found the house to be empty. She returned to her car and called up Harrison. She was finally going to have to take some sort of active approach in learning more about her mother and her life following her time in the psychiatric home.

47

"Hello?" Harrison answered.

"Hey, Harrison. It's Mackenzie. I need you to get some information for me and, if you don't mind, I need you to not make a big deal about it. Tell as few people as you have to."

"I can do that. What do you need?"

"I need to know the cell phone number and current employment status of a Patricia White in Boone's Mill, Nebraska."

"Easy enough. It might take me about fifteen or twenty minutes, though."

"I've got the time. Thanks, Harrison."

She ended the call and sat in the car, looking out at the run-down apartment complex her mother was currently living in. In her line of work, she'd seen much worse but something about her mother living in a ratty apartment complex in a small town where businesses were dying on a weekly basis was depressing.

Patricia White had been the sort of woman who had always yearned for a better life but expected someone to deliver it to her in a nice, pretty package. And when she realized no one was going to bring her such a delivery, she had become an often depressed and brooding woman. Mackenzie had no special memories of spending time with her mother, though she had plenty of memories of her mother drinking a little too much and getting loud and aggressive around the house.

A large part of Mackenzie was glad her mother had ended up in a psychiatric home. Maybe she'd gotten some help. Maybe she had come out a better person. Maybe the person Mackenzie had spoken to on the phone, who still *seemed like* the old Patricia White, was hiding some new evolved qualities.

Not likely, Mackenzie thought with just a bit of bitterness.

As she stared out the window at the parking lot to the apartment complex, her phone rang, startling her. She looked at her watch and saw that she had somehow gotten lost in her thoughts for seventeen minutes.

"Hey, Harrison," she said, answering the call.

"So, I'll text you the number so you can save it to your phone. As for her current working situation, it looks like she's working as a maid at a Holiday Inn in Boone's Mill. Fun little side note—she was also arrested for public intoxication four months ago."

Sounds about right, Mackenzie thought.

"You okay?" Harrison asked.

Realizing that she had been silent for a bit too long, she answered: "Yeah. Thanks again, Harrison."

She ended the call and pulled up the address for the Holiday Inn—the only motel in Boone's Mill. She followed the directions, still undecided if she wanted her mother to be working or not. If she was not working, she'd try the number Harrison had texted her. And if she didn't answer the call, then that would be it. Mackenzie could then tell herself she had tried her best and move on.

Only, she never half-assed anything. If she had to, she'd check herself into the Holiday Inn to make sure she ran into her mother.

The hotel came into view less than ten minutes later after she passed through a sad little town and two of its stoplights. The hotel barely looked more inviting than the apartment complex and there weren't many vehicles in the parking lot. Mackenzie parked, walked inside through the old sliding glass doors, and approached the counter.

A cheerful woman, who was plastered in makeup to make herself look about ten years younger than she actually was, greeted her with a smile. "Welcome! How can I help you today?"

"Is Patricia White working today?"

"She *is*! At this time of the day, she'd be cleaning out rooms. Would you like me to locate her for you?"

"I would," Mackenzie said. She then took out her badge and very subtly slid it across the counter. "It's a private matter. Is there a room I could sit in and wait for her where she and I could speak undisturbed for a while?"

The woman's face grew nearly animated with speculation as she nodded. "Of course. Come on around the counter here and you can use the little break room we have here. Would that suffice?"

"That should be fine."

The woman led Mackenzie down a small hallway just off to the right side of the counter. The break room was situated between a supply closet and an employee restroom. It wasn't the most intimate of places to see her mother for the first time in about twelve years but it would do. Besides…no amount of creature comforts or gentle lighting was going to make the encounter any less miserable.

The woman from the counter went off into the hotel to locate Patricia White. Mackenzie hated that she was so damned nervous. How was it that the thought of speaking with her mother still gave her sweaty palms and a case of the shakes? It made her reconnect far too vividly with her childhood.

She sat at a small square table with five plastic chairs. She tapped her fingers nervously on the table. She spied a coffeemaker on the counter of the small kitchenette and fought the urge to grab a cup for herself. But the last thing she needed before this encounter was more caffeine running through her.

Several minutes later, she heard footsteps coming down the little hallway. She closed her eyes and concentrated. Two sets of them, getting closer. She then opened her eyes as the door opened. The lady from the counter had apparently turned away at the last minute, not wanting to appear nosy.

That left Patricia White, looking through the doorway at a daughter she hadn't seen for a little over twelve years. Mackenzie looked right back at her and for a period of about five seconds nothing happened. No one spoke. No one moved.

Finally, Patricia stepped into the room, closing the door behind her. And even though there was still only silence between them, she approached the table and took a seat.

***

It was eerie how much her mother looked the same. Sure, there were signs of aging but not nearly as bad as Mackenzie had expected. There were slight bags under her eyes and a few gray hairs here and there, but nothing drastically different. Apparently the last twelve years had treated her mother well.

"Why are you here?" Patricia asked, looking across the table at her daughter with a peculiar mix of emotion.

"For work," Mackenzie said dryly, trying to be both real and sarcastic at the same time. "I don't know if you remember or not, but I called you up about a year ago and invited you to a certain graduation."

"I remember," Patricia said. "Felt like I was having my nose rubbed in something."

"Nope. Just trying to reach out and see if you were ready to lay your grudge down."

"I don't have a grudge," Patricia argued.

"No? Then did you just stop giving a damn about the rest of your family once you were ordered to check in to the home? I don't know what things are like with you and Stephanie, but if they're half as bad as they are with me, it's no wonder she's still just sort of stumbling through life."

"That's hardly fair."

"Maybe not. But after twelve years, I think the time for open and honest communication has finally come."

"If that's why you've come all the way out here, you wasted your time. I have nothing to say to you, Mackenzie."

50

"Fortunately, that's *not* the only reason I'm here. Remember, I said I was here for work."

"You're not going to flash your badge?"

"I can, if it makes you feel better," Mackenzie snapped. "But I wouldn't want you to feel like I was rubbing your nose in something."

That comment made Patricia get to her feet and head for the door. She did everything she could not to turn back and face her daughter.

"Mom, stop. There *is* a reason I came by. A pretty big one, actually. Sit down, please."

Patricia turned back to her daughter and slowly took her seat again. There was a slight flicker of fear in her eyes, an unsteadiness that instantly made Mackenzie feel as if in that moment, she had gained full control of the situation.

"There have been a string of recent murders," Mackenzie said. "They go back several months, but the last five have been very recent…all vagrants in the Omaha area."

"Then why in God's name are you way out here?"

"Because we're fairly certain the recent murders are linked to Dad's."

Patricia let out a nervous chuckle, trying her best to seem as if she thought the mere idea of such a thing was bullshit. But that look of fear in her eyes deepened and she was not able to play the part.

"We can't say for certain it's the same person," Mackenzie clarified. "But it's the same kind of gun, the same execution style, the same business card—"

"Stop," Patricia said. She was trembling now and, lo and behold, there were actually tears in her eyes.

"I came by to talk to you because I need to know anything you might remember from that night that you left out in the original investigation. We can't find the killer and right now, honestly, it's almost like he's playing with us. Anything you can think of *at all* would be helpful."

"I told everything I know," she said. "I did it several times seventeen years ago and I'll be damned if I'm going to go through it again. Have you spoken to people in Belton? Half of that stupid town thinks I had something to do with it."

"That might be true," Mackenzie said. "But given the circumstances of that night, it's a sensible rumor. Mom…how much had you had to drink that night?"

Patricia looked as if someone had slapped her in the face. The shock of the question didn't last long, though. It seemed to taper off with the trembling.

"A lot. If you're asking if I was asleep or passed out when your father was killed, the answer is passed out. And before you lay into me about it, you should know that I've beaten myself up plenty over the last few years."

"No. I'm not interested in any of that. I'm doing my absolute best to see you as nothing more than another potential source of information while I'm out here."

"I don't know what to tell you," Patricia said. "I wasn't aware of anything until you came running into the living room and shook me awake. You told me that your dad wasn't moving and I figured he was just asleep. And then you mentioned the blood..."

"I talked to the cop that was in charge of the case at the time," Mackenzie said. "The coroner, too. From what I understand, you were a wreck. A mess. It took you a while to come around and offer your side of the story."

"I was. And quite honestly, I'm glad you don't remember that."

Mackenzie was being as tactful as she could. She needed certain information without making her mother feel as if she was being interrogated. She also felt thrown off of her game by the sheer amount of emotion that was running through her from having her mother sit directly in front of her.

"There were no secrets you kept from me or Stephanie about what happened?" she asked timidly.

"None. Why the hell would I keep anything from you? Or the police for that matter?"

"Well, it wasn't until yesterday that I learned about Dad dabbling in being a landlord before I was born. It was Amy Lucas that told me, by the way."

A genuine smiled crossed Patricia's face. "That was a miserable disaster. He tried it out on a whim...taking out a loan in an effort to dabble in something that he hoped would help get us out of debt. He ended up losing money on it. He was just unprepared for the maintenance demands. We never talked about it because it was stressful. I don't know if you recall, but your father hated to talk about anything he was not good at."

"Well, what about the front door being unlocked?" Mackenzie asked. "I keep hearing how torn up you were about what happened. Was the guilt from the fact that you didn't wake up when the killer came in? That if you hadn't passed out, you might have locked the door before heading to bed?"

Patricia looked up at the ceiling, a frown replacing the smile that had been placed there by the memory of the failed real estate venture.

"Mackenzie," she said, now clearly doing everything she could to not openly weep in front of her daughter. "I don't know what it is you're looking for. But what I do know is that I don't have the strength to rehash it. I spent the last several years investing in myself and making sure the past wouldn't haunt me anymore. So I'm going to respectfully get up from this table and get back to work. If you try asking any more questions, my leaving won't be done so respectfully."

Mackenzie felt her line of questioning dry up in that moment as her mother headed for the door again. Maybe it was because seeing her mother face-to-face made it easier to believe that she was telling the truth. Or maybe it was seeing the pain in her eyes—a woman she had spent the last decade or more hating and begrudging, now visibly nothing more than just a broken person who, just like her, was running from her past.

Whatever the reason, Mackenzie let it go. She did stop her mother one more time as Patricia opened the door to head back to work.

"Mom?"

"What?" Patricia snapped, not looking back at her.

"When this is all over…I'd like to be able to call. I'd like to catch up. Would that be okay with you?" Patricia finally turned back to her. The tears had started to come but she didn't bother trying to hide them. "Yeah. That would be nice."

They left it at that. Mackenzie remained at the table while her mother walked back out into the hallway. She sat there for several moments, collecting her thoughts and her feelings. Sure, the confrontation had been tense and she was coming away with nothing—other than, perhaps, the belief that the rumors that her mother was somehow in on her father's death were unjustified.

She might have sat there for even longer had her phone not buzzed from inside her jacket pocket. She took it out and saw that she had a text from Ellington.

How's it going? the text read.

She almost responded back right away but instead left the break room and headed back down the hallway. She took a quick look around the lobby as she passed by the counter but did not see her mother anywhere. She'd apparently wasted no time in distancing herself from her daughter, back to work cleaning the rooms.

She headed out to her car and started the engine. Before pulling out of the lot and heading back to Belton, she took out her phone and responded to Ellington.

Fine, all things considered. Just met with my mother.

She waited a moment, sure that Ellington would respond back right away. He didn't text often and when he did, he preferred to finish a conversation rather than having one lag on for hours. When he responded, it was in typical Ellington fashion.

Holy shit. Are you okay?

Yeah, she responded. **You?**

Nothing new down here. Going over all vagrant cases. Dead ends all around. When you coming back?

She sighed and tossed her phone in the passenger seat. The truth was, she didn't know when she was heading back. But she didn't want to let Ellington know that. She found herself annoyed with him again—wishing he was here, wishing he had chosen to come out here with her.

Hell, maybe she'd go back right now. Maybe she'd go back to Belton just to check out of her room and then drive back to Omaha.

It seemed like the most plausible idea but when she started driving forward, she realized that she was shaking. Also, there were tears lurking somewhere under the surface and she knew she wouldn't be able to keep them away for long.

As a matter of fact, the first one escaped the corner of her eye just after she pulled away from the Holiday Inn and headed back toward the town where she had grown up.

CHAPTER ELEVEN

On the way back to Belton, she decided she'd get a few hours of sleep and then check out around four in the morning. That would put her back in Omaha at nine or ten in the morning, giving her a full day to wave herself back into the flow of things.

She noticed along the way that Ellington did not try to get her to answer his last text. She was trying to figure out why she was so annoyed with him. She'd been angry with him before but she usually had a discernable reason. Maybe it was just the case clouding her judgment. Now that she'd faced down her mother, she'd be able to figure out the source of her irritation when she was with him again.

She got back to her room at 4:45 and ordered from the town's only Chinese restaurant. As she waited for her food, she showered and changed into jeans and a T-shirt. She opened her laptop, took out all of the files she had pertaining to the case, and was soon digging into both the case and a plate of orange chicken.

She added some notes to her digital files, adding in some of the details that the coroner and Reggie Thompson had told her about. As she added each note, she went over them in her head as if she were standing in the middle of some imagined crime scene.

Speculation that he was undercover, working on a drug case. Also rumored that Jimmy Scotts had some connection to a drug cartel out of Mexico. It's a link but, in the case of Scotts, was dismissed after some pretty strict field work.

Police investigation dropped seemingly out of nowhere, but why? Orders from higher-ups? Were officers getting too close to some truth that might cause issues?

Coroner reports nothing out of the ordinary. Gunshot to the head from point-blank range, no question.

With the notes updated, it was clear that there were still many directions for the case to go. The worst part of it all was that she did not feel like she was making any progress.

With her dinner eaten and the case beginning to feel stale, Mackenzie went into one of her bags and pulled out a small bottle of melatonin. She kept it on her for cases where she was unable to sleep, usually only needing it when she had overstretched herself and was hitting her second or third wind.

She took it just before eight; while it was early, her hope was that she'd spring awake around three and get an hour head start back to Omaha. She toyed with the idea of leaving right there and then but knew it would mean she'd be ragged and tired all of tomorrow.

She settled into bed, hoping the aid of the melatonin would keep the nightmares away.

When she was startled awake some time later, she was pleased to find she had enjoyed a dream-free sleep but was also filled with the knowledge that a phone call at such an hour was never anything good…especially in her line of work.

She fumbled for her cell phone and saw that it was Ellington. She was too startled and groggy to be annoyed as she answered with a soft and weary: "Hello?"

"Hey, Mac," he said. "Sorry to call you so late. Or early. Or whatever. But I really need to know when you can get back here."

"Why? What's up?"

"There's been another murder. Another vagrant. And this one's fresh. I'm headed to the crime scene with Penbrook right now. Based on what we know, the murder can't have occurred any more than an hour ago."

"Shit," Mackenzie said, quickly snapping awake. She looked to the clock and saw that it was 2:15.

"Don't kill yourself trying to get here," he said. "But yeah…get here as soon as you can."

"I'm on it," she said. "Can you text me the crime scene address?"

"Yeah."

She wanted to keep talking to him, to hear his voice as she came fully awake. But there was no time for sentimentality…or for whatever weird repressed anger she had been feeling toward him since leaving Omaha. So she settled for "I'll see you in a bit" before killing the call.

She took some time to go to the bathroom to splash some water in her face. She then gathered everything into her bags and headed to the main office. The man behind the desk was snoozing in a chair with a book in his lap. Mackenzie rapped her knuckles against the counter, stirring him awake.

As he checked her out of her room, Mackenzie hurried over to the little coffee nook that sat between the counter and the entrance to the not-yet-open complimentary breakfast section. She grabbed a cup of coffee, took her receipt from the clerk, and headed out for her car.

Less than ten minutes after Ellington had called, Mackenzie was on the road, heading back to Omaha. She felt okay with the move, as she sensed there was nothing more in Belton for her. She'd come out here, did what she had intended to do, and yet had yielded no real results. But now at least she knew.

Also, she had faced a ghost that had haunted her forever—a ghost in the form of her mother. She had come out of it fine and basically unscarred.

And something about that placed a feeling of hope within her. Whether for the case or for her ability to move on from the chains that had held her to her past, she did not know.

CHAPTER TWELVE

A drive that should have taken her six hours ended up only taking a little over five. As she had passed through each individual county, she had called the local PDs, gave them her badge number and the license plate number of her rental, and informed them that she was speeding back to Omaha. She arrived just before 7:30 in the morning, the speedy trip having invigorated her.

The crime scene was located behind an old grocery store—a Super Saver, if Mackenzie was reading the faded logo on the front of the building correctly. She parked her car alongside the few others that were just in front of a section of cracked and faded parking lot that had been cordoned off with yellow crime scene tape. As she parked, she saw Ellington speaking into a cell phone amidst several other men, some of whom were dressed in standard bureau suit attire.

She ducked under the crime scene tape and headed for Ellington. She took in the scene as she crossed the lot and found herself looking at what appeared to be some sort of derelict camping ground. There were sheets and old bundled sleeping bags pressed against the back of the building. Empty glass bottles and other trash remnants were scattered around. All signs of a miniature vagrant camp.

Ellington saw her approaching and promptly ended the call he was on. "Hey," he said with a subtle yearning in his eyes. He was glad to see her, glad to have her back. But there was hesitation there, too.

"Hey. Was that Penbrook?" she asked, pointing to Ellington's phone.

"It was," he said. "He's back at the office, working with forensics."

"You mind filling me in?" she asked as she looked at the small crowd of bureau figures behind them. There were four in all, chattering together and comparing notes. Another was off to the side, questioning a man in a stained puffy coat.

"Yeah. Pretty simple. The local PD called the field office around two in the morning. This man right here," he said, pointing to the man in the puffy coat, "called us using a burner phone. He

58

apparently sleeps here. He said someone came along with a gun and told them he had a tough choice to make. He then proceeded to undergo a literal round of eeney, meeney, miney, mo. The body over there," he said, pointing to a shape under a black tarp to the left, "was the unfortunate man that was picked."

"And that's it?"

"No, not exactly," Ellington said. He then held his hand out to her. There was a plastic bag in his hand. Inside the bag there was a business card that read **Barker Antiques**. "This was found right in the middle of the lot. Like *right* in the center, as if it was placed there with great care and precision."

Mackenzie eyed the card and felt like she had swallowed a lead weight. She almost reached out for it but had no interest in touching it. She'd spent far too much of the last year of her life obsessing over that damned card.

"What happened after he shot the victim?" she asked.

"Then the man left."

"No one saw his face?"

"Nope. If you want, we can question our friend over there," Ellington said, pointing to the man in the coat again. "He seems happy to be getting all of the attention."

Mackenzie wasted no time in heading over to where the man— clearly a vagrant from the clothes he wore to the state of his hair and skin. She unapologetically cut off the agent who was already speaking to him. She figured Penbrook had given her full sway over the case, so she'd take advantage of it.

"Sorry," she said, clearly not meaning it. "I'd like a few minutes with him." She did not ask if it was okay; she simply waited for the agent to take his leave, which he did after several moments.

The vagrant looked at Mackenzie and then at Ellington. She could smell sour liquor on him, along with the stench of dirt and sweat.

"You saw what happened?" Mackenzie asked.

"I did," the man said enthusiastically. "I was only one finger point from getting shot. We were all sleeping right there along that wall and this man comes in with a gun like he owned the place."

"Were you able to see his face?" Mackenzie asked.

"Nope. He was wearing a mask. Like one of those cheap Halloween masks. Nothing spooky, just a white mask. Like you sometimes see on a theater poster."

"How many of you were there when he approached?"

"Five of us."

"So where are the other three?"

"They hauled ass as soon as the guy left. One of them even searched the poor dead bastard's pockets when they left." He stopped here to think for a moment and then added: "Shit, I don't even know the guy's name."

"No one does yet," Ellington added, speaking directly to Mackenzie. "It's one of the things we're actively trying to figure out."

"So what else can you tell us?" Mackenzie asked. "Any details will be fine. Anything at all, even if you think it's just a small detail we wouldn't care about."

"Nothing. We're just all scared, you know. We've been hearing about this for weeks now…this asshole going around killing homeless people. All I remember is the mask and the gun and then the gunshot. I ran…ran behind a building two blocks down where I used to sleep before the fucking cops got on me about it. Then I called the police on my phone."

No means to live in a house, but he has a cell phone, Mackenzie thought. *Great priorities.*

"Do you recall how tall the man was? Maybe if he was thin or overweight?"

"Well, he wasn't very tall at all. Maybe average height. And not overweight. Just an average build, I guess."

"What was he wearing, other than the mask?"

"Jeans, I think. And a long-sleeved black shirt. He was wearing gloves, too. I saw them when he put the gun to that guy's head."

"So you didn't see his skin color?" Ellington asked.

"I did, actually," the man said. "Between the collar of his shirt and that mask. His neck and jaw. He was a white dude. Sort of a deep voice, too."

"Anything else?"

"Nah. Just that…shooting that guy didn't seem to bother him at all. He pulled the trigger, watched the dude drop, and then just walked off like nothing had happened."

"And no one bothered chasing him?" Mackenzie asked.

"Hell no. He had a gun. And after what we'd just seen, the dude was clearly off his rocker, you know?"

Mackenzie looked back at the scene, to the shape under the tarp.

That makes five vagrants in less than two weeks, she thought. *He's moving fast. He's almost daring us to find him…and if we don't this is going to get out of control.*

60

"You want to head back to the field office?" Ellington asked. "Penbrook is setting up a debrief meeting that's taking place in an hour."

"Yeah," she said, already starting back for the car.

Ellington raced to catch up with her. "You okay?" he asked.

"I'm fine."

"Okay. So…are *we* okay?"

"Yes," she said. "And I apologize if I acted in a way that made you think we weren't."

"It's cool," he said. "I can't even begin to imagine what revisiting all of this is doing to you. If I'm being honest, I'm a little pissed at McGrath for letting you run with this."

She shrugged. "I think he sensed I wouldn't shut up until the case was mine." She opened her car door and nodded to the passenger side. "Want to catch a ride with me?"

"Yeah, that sounds good."

It felt good to have him there again, by her side. There was a tension between them but it wasn't anything they would not be able to handle. For now, she just dwelled on the fact that she felt whole again—that if she happened to stumble and fall along the way, Ellington would be there to help her back up.

She pulled out of the lot and back out onto the street. Ellington reached out and took her hand and even in his slight touch, something felt different.

You'd better quickly learn to better separate your work life from your love life, she told herself. *If you don't, this case is going to wreck you.*

CHAPTER THIRTEEN

By the time she returned to the field office, grabbed a cup of coffee, and headed to the conference room, the debrief meeting was being assembled. People were milling in and out of the conference room with a speed and efficiency that usually only occurred when a case was about to be wrapped. She liked the energy and enthusiasm but at the same time, it all felt wasted.

Fearing that she would seem like the gray storm cloud on their motivation, Mackenzie hung back in the far corner of the room. She grabbed a copy of the preliminary findings from this morning's scene and looked them over while Penbrook and a few others came into the room. Ellington sat beside her and while she was still enjoying the sense of him near her, there was also a small part of her that wanted to go at this whole thing alone. She felt she owed it to herself and that Ellington would end up being nothing more than a bystander.

It was talking to Mom, she thought. *Talking to her and realizing that, despite her faults, her hands are clean in this case, and I'm more motivated than ever to wrap it.*

She caught Ellington looking at her, giving her a thin smile. He knew her well—when she needed space and when she needed to be challenged. She appreciated this about him and, again, it reminded her of how she had fallen for him so quickly after the initial physical attraction had swept them up. Knowing the state she was in, he was opting to let her ride this out as if it were just any old case.

After another few moments, Penbrook had someone close the door and then he took position at the head of the table. He stayed on his feet, opting not to sit down, and looked like nothing more than a bundle of nervous energy. So far he had not spoken a single word to Mackenzie. It made her wonder just how pissed off he truly was with her for going out to Morrill County for two days.

"Okay, okay, take a seat, everyone," Penbrook loudly said. The dozen or so people within the room all sat down and the conversation died down to a murmur and then nothing.

He then took about two minutes to fill everyone in the room in on the events that had occurred behind the old grocery store in the early morning hours. The story he told lined up exactly with the events the homeless man had told Mackenzie no more than fifty minutes ago.

"As of right now," he added when he was done with recounting the scene, "we still don't know the man's name. There was no ID on him but that could be because another of the vagrants in the area reportedly picked his pockets after he was killed and then fled the scene. We know nothing about this man other than the fact that he was killed in the exact same manner as the other vagrants. From the point-blank execution to the business card, it's all the same. Right now, here is all we have."

With that, he went through a few slides of the scene. Mackenzie scoured each one, hoping for some sort of clue or sign that she had missed when she had been there before. But there was nothing. Absolutely nothing.

"What about the mask?" one of the agents at the table asked. "If it was a unique mask, we could narrow a search down to costume shops."

"From what we're being told by eyewitnesses, it was a very basic drama mask," Penbrook said. "That means we'd be looking at every Walmart and dollar store in the state."

The room was quiet for a moment as Penbrook finished cycling through the slides. When he was done, he turned to face Mackenzie. There was a very subtle smirk on his face that felt a little confrontational to Mackenzie.

"Were you able to uncover anything on your trek out to Morrill County?"

It was a blatant way to challenge her in front of the gathered crowd. She saw Ellington out of the corner of her eye. He cringed, though she was sure it was not for her. He knew her well enough to know what was coming after such a challenge.

"I did, actually," she said. Although the few things she did discover were rather insignificant, she figured she could paint them as larger clues if she needed to. And after calling her out in such a way, that was exactly what she'd do if she had to.

"Care to share?" Penbrook asked.

"Well, I started at the beginning…with the murder of Benjamin White, my father. As the broader case file shows, he was the first murder reported in this manner…shot at point-blank range in the back of the head with the business card present. Jimmy Scotts and Gabriel Hambry would later be killed the same way. I spoke to the policeman that oversaw my father's case and he spoke about how the case was going nowhere but they kept pushing it along. Then, out of nowhere, the case was basically ignored. It was a demand that came down from on high and no real reason was ever given.

"There were, however, rumors that my father was working undercover in an attempt to bust up a drug ring that was based out of Mexico. It's been assumed that his murder was linked to that but it's too convenient...especially if the killer is now killing vagrants."

"So nothing new, then," Penbrook said.

"In the long run, no. Tell me, though...what case-breaking information did you obtain here while I was gone for two days? You had a whole team at your side. Surely you found something while I was apparently wasting my time."

"I didn't say that, Agent White. And I'd appreciate it if we can stay on point here."

"I'm sure you would," she said.

And then, moving before she was fully aware of what she was doing, she grabbed her briefing report and stood up from the table. She then marched to the door in a sheet of silence. She could feel everyone's eyes on her until she was out of the room and closing the door behind her—especially Ellington's.

She paced down the hall when she slowly started to realize that although Penbrook's challenge had been borderline bully-like behavior, her reaction had also been a little childish.

To hell with it, she thought. *Even if he calls McGrath to complain, which I doubt he will because he essentially challenged me in front of our peers, the worst I'll get is a slap on the wrist.*

More frustrated than ever, she took the elevator down to the lobby and went out to her rental car. She had no idea where she was going to go or what she was going to do. She just had to be alone with her thoughts, away from people for a while. She knew deep in her heart that she had not allowed herself enough time to process having briefly met her mother. It was still tugging at her and driving just about every decision she made—both logical and emotional. And until this case was closed, she was afraid that would continue to happen.

No leads. No clues. No potential avenues to take. This entire thing is just one huge dead end.

And the worst part of it was that because she had still never shared everything about her past with Ellington, she could not process it all with him. Because even if she *could* somehow break apart her professional life and her emotional life, no one knew her private thoughts about the death of her father and the tentacles of hatred this case seemed to be gripping her with. Essentially, she was alone, like she had wanted when she left the debriefing. All alone, with no one to talk to.

Only…that might not be completely true.

She picked up her phone and looked at it for a moment. She scrolled through her contacts and paused at a number she had not used in a while—at a name she honestly hadn't even considered for quite some time.

When she pressed CALL, she felt desperate and a little lost. But with absolutely no sign of this case coming to a close anytime soon, maybe she *was* desperate.

That being the case, she was willing to seek help wherever she could find it.

CHAPTER FOURTEEN

She had not spoken to Samuel McClarren for nearly six months. She'd nearly worshipped the man when she had been working her way through the academy. More than that, he had served as a reassuring voice—almost like a mentor—when the pressure had really been applied when she had been given the title of Agent. She respected the hell out of the man and that was why she felt so embarrassed when he answered her call on the fourth ring.

"Unless my caller ID deceives me," McClarren said, "this is the infamous Mackenzie White. But surely she'd have no reason to call me, an old washed up educator."

"Oh, it's me, all right," she said. "And you are far from a washed up educator."

It was true. Despite his humble attitude McClarren had written several influential texts on the mindsets and mannerisms of serial killers. The man was a genius when it came to how the human mind worked, particularly when it came to the violent and miscreant. It also didn't hurt that he had been one hell of an agent back in his day—an agent who had been promoted to deputy director before retiring and then teaching at the academy.

"Well, I have to tell myself those things so I don't get a big head. Now…if you'll forgive me for saying so, I'm assuming you haven't called because you want to catch up. I've been keeping up with your work record and I'd imagine you don't have time to simply make a few friendly calls to chat."

"Sadly enough, that's correct," Mackenzie said.

"Nothing sad about that," McClarren said. "You're racking up one hell of an impressive track record. I assume you're in the midst of an investigation now, correct?"

"Correct. And honestly, I could use some insight. Some pointers from someone removed from the case that knows how an agent thinks. Because right now I'm just too mired in the case. It's too personal to me."

"Is everything okay?" he asked. "Are you on a case with personal ties? Because you know that can be very dangerous."

"I know," she said. "But this one is a little different."

She then went on to tell him about the case. She started, though, with the deaths of Jimmy Scotts and Gabriel Hambry and how they aligned with the murder of her father. She then went into the murder of Dennis Parks and the vagrant killings. It took longer than she thought and each and every fact came to her mind easily because of the time and obsession she had put into it.

"Yeah, I've heard murmurs of this case," he said. "I didn't know about the business cards, though. That's a strange little tidbit."

"Well, to make it even stranger, I found one on my windshield in DC," Mackenzie said. "It was right around the time I started to realize that getting assigned to this case might eventually be a reality."

"So you think it was used as a scare tactic? Someone trying to intimidate you to stay away from the case and nothing more?"

"Yeah, there was even a message on it, telling me to stay away from the case. *Stop looking,* it said."

"Seems strange, doesn't it?" McClarren said. "If the killer is in Nebraska, why would he come to DC just to place a business card on your car? If he traveled that far, you'd think he might have tried something more drastic."

It was something Mackenzie had thought about a few times but had not really dedicated much time to. But now that she was speaking with McClarren—to have someone actually voice it as well—she realized how asinine the gesture was. If it was a scare tactic, it was a weak one. And given the fact that this man had already killed at least eight people, including her father, she was sure he wasn't beyond using extreme measures to scare her.

"I considered that it might just be a prank," she said. "There were a lot of other students in the academy that were pissed that I was cherry-picked."

"So...here's the thing," McClarren said. "I'm sixty-three this year. And sadly, wisdom does not always come with old age. I don't have a crystal ball that I can rub or anything like that. But in a case that spans back this far and has so many different parts to it, there is one approach I can suggest."

"Please," she said. "I'd appreciate it."

"If you think of the case as a puzzle, as I'm sure you were taught to do at some point in your training, you can sort of prioritize it. Some people find the edge pieces first. Some people find one patch of a solid color and start working on that first. There's no one right way to put a puzzle together. And it's even harder to put the puzzle together if some jerk has accidentally put pieces from another puzzle into your puzzle box. All that to say...well, sometimes the pieces that don't fit just don't fit. No matter how hard you press it down or tell yourself the colors *do* match, the piece just won't fit. You follow me?"

"Yes," she said, loving the way the man could use an analogy.

"So look at your case—at your puzzle—and ask yourself: which of these pieces doesn't belong in your box? Which of these pieces doesn't fit?"

A small smile came to her lips. "Thank you," she said. "And I'm sorry I called. I just...I feel lost."

"Oh, it's okay. It's nice to feel wanted. You're free to call me anytime. So long as that hard-ass McGrath doesn't have an issue with it."

"I'll do that," she said.

"And just hold out, Agent White. I've been following your record and it's stellar so far. You've got something I can't name...something most agents don't have. You'll get this one, too. Bye now."

He ended the call there, signing off in a way that let her know that this was her deal to break now. Sure, his advice had been rather subtle and vague, but she understood it perfectly.

Which piece doesn't fit?

She kept going back to the business card that had been left on her car. It had been so ominous and so perfectly timed that she had assumed it must have been from the killer or an associate of the killer. Honestly, a large part of her still felt that way.

But now...

She pulled up another name on her phone, one she had called fairly frequently in the past few weeks: Harrison. As dutiful as ever, he answered right away.

"Harrison...where are you right now?"

"Sitting at my cubicle. Why?"

"I need you to do me a favor. I need you to go into my office. On the base of the lamp is the business card I found on my car a month or so ago. You know the one I'm talking about?"

"Oh yeah."

"I've got a weird request, but the sooner you can get me results, the happier I'll be."

"I don't mind weird requests," Harrison said. "Whatcha got?"

She smiled. It was good to hear him happy. He'd been in a funk ever since his mother died and he had been reassigned back to his normal grunt work and desk duty. "I want you to take that card to

Forensics. See if they can figure out how old it is, when it was printed."

"I can do that."

"Put some urgency on it. See what you can do to make it top priority. I'm pretty sure McGrath would have my back on this."

They ended the call and Mackenzie realized that in the time the two calls had taken—less than fifteen minutes total—she had managed to deescalate her emotional meltdown. She opened her car door, prepared to go back inside and perhaps pull Ellington to the side to try to explain her mood. Hell, maybe she'd even apologize to Penbrook.

But then another thought occurred to her—something she felt almost foolish for not thinking of yesterday. It was a thin thread of hope, but it was hope nonetheless.

She closed the car door, started the engine, and headed back to the motel. On the way, she Googled the number for the Belton police department and made a request she hoped the little station was equipped to handle.

***

The filing cabinets and carpet in the Belton police station had been outdated when she had visited, but their Internet was up to speed. She'd called and requested to have any files pertaining to the deaths of homeless people and/or vagrants emailed to her. The woman she spoke to explained that they had not yet fully converted to digital files and some of the records would have to be scanned, saved as PDFs, and emailed. She was promised results within two or three hours.

However, by the time she was back in her motel room and setting up her laptop, she had already received two files from the Belton station. She felt almost guilty for sitting alone in her motel room at ten o'clock in the morning, sipping on a coffee and eating a cheese Danish, but not enough to stop working.

On two separate occasions, Ellington texted her. One read: **Where the hell did you go?** The second read: **Call me before this gets out of hand.**

She ignored both of the messages as she looked over the first two files.

One file told the story of a drifter who had come into town in 1985. A mechanic had hired him for some under the table work. He'd become an unofficial resident, sometimes sleeping in the garage the mechanic owned but more often than not found passed out, black-out drunk, behind Belton Grocery. He was killed two months after coming into town, the victim of a stab wound to the gut when he tried to rob a teenager late at night.

Strike one, she thought.

The second file was much simpler. In 2007, a body had been discovered in a pond just outside of the Belton town limits. After a week or so of searching, the man's identity pointed to a small town just outside of Lincoln. The autopsy showed an insane amount of heroin in his system and rope burns around his ankles and wrists. No gunshot to the head. No mention of a business card.

Strike two.

As she wrapped this one up, she got one last email from the Belton PD. It came with one attachment and a brief message within the body of the email. The message read: *We had two people digging through the files and this third one is it. Three cases concerning vagrants since 1980. Do we need to go farther back?*

Mackenzie replied back with a *no* and gave her thanks for their prompt hard work. She then opened the file, though its meager file size told her the report would be brief and likely not what she was looking for. The file told the story of a man who had picked up a hitchhiker in 1992. Some sort of scuffle had broken out between the two and the driver had kicked the man out of the car. When the hitchhiker threw rocks at the car, the driver backed up, intending to just scare the guy, but ended up slamming right into him. He died forty minutes later on the way to the hospital.

Strike three, Mackenzie thought. *You're out.*

As she signed out of her email and tried to prepare herself to head back to the field office, her cell phone rang. When she saw that it was Harrison, she answered it right away.

"What did you find out?" she asked.

"Well…I'm being told that such a rushed test can only provide estimates. So let me tell you that right now. That being said, Forensics is telling me that this card was definitely printed sometime in the last five years or so."

"Did you say *five?*"

"That's right. And there's more. We figured you were trying to compare it to the ones from Nebraska. So I pulled the files from those cases—your dad, Gabriel Hambry, Jimmy Scotts, and Dennis Parks. The font is the same but the hue of the ink is off. It's two different shades of black."

"So it wasn't from the original printing," she said. "It's a fake."

"Seems like it," Harrison said. "You should know that McGrath caught wind of this. Forensics gave me shit when I asked to have it expedited, so they reached out to him to confirm. He's pissed...not about the test, but that someone was apparently messing with you. He's got your back on this."

"What do you mean?"

"Someone duped you, White. He's actively trying to figure out who."

She was flushed with a weird sense of security at this. If McGrath had ever looked out for her in such a way before, she sure as hell had not been aware of it.

"Thanks, Harrison."

"That's what I'm here for," he said. He spoke it with a bit of sarcasm, though—an underlying note of resentment that he was riding a desk while she was all over the country.

She ended the call and thought about the day she had found that card on her windshield. She'd been scared and shaken. It had thrown her off and it had made her feel as if she had been out of her depth.

She suddenly wished she was back in DC. She'd love to take part in the hunt for the asshole that had played this trick on her.

Was it a trick, though? she asked herself. *This killer's work spans back almost twenty years. Maybe he's deep enough into his work that he knows I'm on to him. Is it so impossible to believe that he has connections?*

It felt flimsy, but until she was proven otherwise, it was something she was willing to consider. For now, she just had to wait.

And waiting was not something she did well. With a sigh and a final gulp of coffee that had gone cold, Mackenzie left her room and once again headed back out to her car. She'd have to suck it up and get back to the field office. She could take the nasty stares from Penbrook and his sycophants. But the thing with Ellington...she wasn't too sure. Deep down, she knew that he was only trying to help her—that he *needed* to help her.

And for reasons she was still not able to define, she realized she did not want his help. Or, rather, she *did* but would not admit it. And that was a whole different, much deeper conversation.

She wasn't sure if she was ready to deal with that.

As she got into her car, her cell phone rang. She thought it might be Harrison calling to tell her that McGrath had already cracked a guy and got a confession. But when she looked at the Caller ID, the name she saw there stunned her.

Kirk Peterson.

She answered the call with a bit of anxiety, recalling the state the rattled detective had been in the last time she had spoken with him. "Hello? Peterson, is this you?"

"Yeah," he said. "You sound surprised."

"I'm...well, I'm just remembering your state the last time we spoke."

"Yeah. That was rough. It's a little better now. But that's neither here nor there. Look, I caught wind that you were in Belton earlier. That true?"

"Yeah, why?"

"Just curious. Find anything?"

"Hardly," she answered.

"Well, where are you now? In Omaha again?"

"Good guess."

"Listen...how soon can you meet me? A quick meeting, nothing formal. There are some things I should maybe tell you—things I was too fucked up to get around to last time I saw you. You got the time?"

"Tell me when and where, and I'll make it happen. The sooner the better."

On the other end of the line, Peterson chuckled and then told her when and where.

CHAPTER FIFTEEN

She met with Kirk Peterson for a very late lunch at a Tex-Mex place just twenty minutes away from the field office. It was ideal because she hadn't really eaten much of anything over the last day or so, just snacking on pastries whenever she managed to get coffee. When she entered the place and saw Peterson sitting in a booth in the back, she joined him.

She was glad to see that he had been telling the truth about his current state. He did indeed look better. The five o'clock shadow on his face looked intentional rather than neglected. He was wearing casual clothes—a hoodie and a pair of jeans with a baseball cap— but still looked clean. Mostly, though, the recovery she saw came from his eyes and the expression he gave her when she sat down across from him. Whatever had been bugging him when she'd last met him (the death of a vagrant child, if he was to be believed) had apparently been handled.

"You're looking much better," she said.

"Thanks. It wasn't hard. Anything would be better than the miserable state you saw me in a few weeks ago."

"What changed it?" she asked.

"I made myself stop drinking, first of all. And then I realized that the only way to escape the things I've seen and the ways I've failed was to do something about it."

"So you're picking the case back up?" she asked.

"Not exactly. And honestly, I think if I tried, the bureau would likely roadblock me based on the way I had been behaving. And maybe that's for the best."

"Then why call me?" she asked.

"Because while I may not really want to delve back into the depths of the case, there *is* some information that I think might be pertinent. And honestly, I'd much rather you have it than Penbrook. He's a good agent but….well, I know how close you are to this case. And it could just be a coincidence, anyway…"

"Seems like you're stalling."

"I might be," he said. "Order something. Let's eat."

She wanted to push him, to get the information right away. But she also knew that if he was recovering from a way in which this case had affected him, she needed to act with kid gloves. She figured she could allow him a few minutes of just feeling normal—of enjoying the feeling that he had someone he could vent to.

They ordered their food and Mackenzie even allowed herself the rare daytime beer. For the next twenty minutes, over a burrito and a Dos Equis, she caught him up on where she was in the case. She did her best to not get into the details of how McGrath had worked behind the scenes to make sure she got it and Peterson seemed to pick up on that, leaving all of the obvious questions unturned.

He seemed genuinely interested in her stories and, though it made her feel a bit conceited, she was fairly certain he was also just interested in *her*. It was in the way he looked at her, the way he leaned in a bit across the table when he responded to things she said. It was nice to know that despite the mess she felt she kept herself in, men still found her attractive. Of course, she felt that way with Ellington most of the time—something she hoped was not on the line after the way she'd been acting. So appreciating the attention of another man might complicate things even more.

It was that feeling (and her now-empty beer) that pushed her toward getting the information out of him. Besides…he seemed to practically be bursting at the seams to share what he knew.

"Okay, so coincidence or not…what do you have, Peterson?"

"Kirk, please," he said.

"Fine. Kirk."

"Well, after I met you the first time, when you and I went out to Jimmy Scotts's residence and then to the house where you grew up, I found myself eyeing the case with you in mind. I started seeing you as a next of kin rather than an agent that was investigating the case. And when I did that, it seemed that a lot of other doors in my head opened up and I was able to dig a little deeper.

"So, about four days after you came by last time—when I was in my wrecked state—I started from square one with these vagrants. I got together every piece of information on them I could find. Some of the information was easy to come by while some of it was being held like some closely guarded secret by the bureau. But thanks to some old friends on the State Police, I was able to get most of what I wanted."

"Good to see that the State Police haven't changed much since I was dealing with them as a detective," she said.

"Yeah, some things stay very much the same," he said. "Anyway…one of the things I started looking at were phone records. Homeless or not, I'm sure you've noticed that a big part of the homeless community have those shitty burner phones. It's like ten bucks for a month of service on this plastic phone. Better than any deal I ever got from my provider."

He'd been going for a laugh but when he saw that she was strictly in work-focus mode, he shrugged the failed attempt off and carried on.

"The phone records of the vagrants were quite easy to go through. Of the deceased, only three had those phones. Of the three, one only made calls to his sister and one of those late night AM radio conspiracy shows. The other guy, though, had a pretty extensive calling history. This was a guy by the name of Clarence Biggs. I looked back through the two months he'd had the phone and there were calls to seventeen different people. One of those people was a man named Trevor Black. That name mean anything to you?"

"No. Should it?"

"I don't know. But I think it will by the time you leave here. See…I ran down fourteen of the seventeen people that Clarence Biggs had called. A few were family. Another was some sort of welfare program he had applied to. But in the mix of all of it was a guy named Trevor Black. At first when I talked to him, it seemed like a dead end. But I then did some digging on him and three other people I spoke with who had been on Clarence Biggs's call history. And when I dug far enough into Trevor Black, I came up with a pretty solid connection."

"A connection to what?" Mackenzie asked.

"To you."

"That name doesn't ring any bells," she said, frantically searching her mind.

"Maybe not. But I bet it would ring some bells for your sister. She dated Trevor Black for about six months. They broke up less than a year ago."

"My sister?" Mackenzie asked, incredulous. "Are you sure?"
"Yeah. According to Trevor anyway. When I reached out to your sister, she was pretty fucking rude."

"Yeah, that's Stephanie. Did you lead in with the fact that you knew me?"

"I did."

"That's probably why she was so rude."

"Now here's where it gets messed up," Kirk said. "Trevor Black spoke to me a single time. It was a fruitful conversation but

I'm sure you could have an even better one with him. If you could, that is."

"And why can't I?"

"He was killed last week. He lives out in California, out near Napa. He died in one of those freak forest fires. Crappy luck on your part, huh?"

"And his," she conceded. She found that she liked interacting with Peterson in this unofficial sort of way. There was a nice banter here, making her think that in his heyday, he might have actually been a damned good detective.

"Anyway, his story checks out. He did date your sister. When I asked for proof, he was sort of crude. He talked about a scar…"

"On her upper left thigh," Mackenzie said. "Yeah…a motorcycle accident when she was nineteen. What else did he say about her?"

"That she wasn't really into commitment. He left her because she was having sex with someone else at the same time. Also, I think her…um, her *career* got in the way."

"She's a stripper," Mackenzie said. "Or, she *was* the last time I spoke with her. Which has been about a year or so."

She sighed and tried to keep her mind on track. Surely it couldn't be a coincidence that her sister had been dating a man who had apparently been in contact with one of the murdered vagrants, right? It seemed even less like a coincidence when she considered that Dennis Parks had also been recently killed—a man who had once known her father quite well.

You're going to have to talk to her, she thought. *First your mom and now Stephanie. Man…this really did turn out to be one hell of a homecoming, didn't it?*

"I'm right to have shared this with you, aren't I?" he asked. "I mean…there's a fine line between work and personal life on this sort of thing…"

"Absolutely," she said. "It just means I'm going to have to finally break down and talk to my damned sister again. Did you get *anything* out of her?"

"No. She literally refused to talk to me. I tried telling her I knew you and then that I had been working towards finding the man that killed her father and—"

"Oooh, yeah, not good. She's never dealt with it." She shrugged and chuckled, tempted to have another beer. "It's an interesting family dynamic. What about Trevor Black? Did he tell you why he was in contact with the vagrant?"

"He claimed he got a call from the number and didn't recognize it, so he called it back. When he found out it was apparently a wrong number, that was that. But I don't buy it because the call he made back to the number lasted about five minutes. And you don't call a wrong number and just chat, you know?"

"That *is* weird. I mean, I don't mind conceding a few things here and there to being just coincidental, but this goes a bit beyond that point."

"Trevor *did* say the homeless guy was pretty chatty. That makes sense, I guess, as maybe a homeless guy was just happy to have someone to talk to. But…five minutes?"

"Yeah…it's strange."

"I thought so, too," Kirk said. Before he could say anything else, a waitress came by. He ordered another beer and another taco and then resumed when the waitress was gone. "Your sister…where does she live?"

"The last I heard, she wasn't too far away from here. Kansas City. Been there for a few years. It was like she wanted to get away from home, but not too far. She was never one to fully separate herself from drama."

"You think you might pay her a visit?" he asked.

She nodded but then shrugged, not sure how to respond. She reached into her wallet, grabbed a twenty, and tossed it on the table. "I need to get going. This is…well, this a lot to process."

"After you've talked to her, do you need someone to process it with?"

She smiled at him and had to admit to herself that she did like the attention. "I sort of already *do* have someone like that."

He nodded and looked down at the table. "I figured. But hey…worth a shot, right?"

"Always," she said. "Thanks for the information."

"Anytime."

She left, feeling disconnected and a little chagrined. She wasn't at all surprised that a visit back to Nebraska was going to lead to a visit to her estranged sister. She'd like to think that after meeting with her mother, it might not be so bad. But she wasn't that naïve when it came to her family.

When she got into her car, she also realized that family drama was about to get in the way of the case. And not only was that unprofessional, it was a great way to veer her mind away from the central point—and that was closing this case once and for all.

With no clear path to take and several open-ended questions still waiting for closure, she saw no better approach than to head back to the field office to reconnect with Ellington. With her head and her heart in chaos, she headed in that direction. She felt herself sliding toward despair—about things with her sister, with the case, with Ellington. It was just all too much to handle at once.

She started to wonder what a nervous breakdown felt like when her phone rang. Seeing that it was Harrison, she answered it at once.

"We got him," Harrison said before Mackenzie could speak a word.

"You're sure?"

"Pretty damned positive," Harrison said. "Yardley brought him in and is about to take him into interrogation with McGrath. McGrath wants to know if you're in a place where you might be able to live-stream it. He wants your take on it."

"I'm about ten minutes away from the field office. Set things up on your end and I'll call as soon as I can."

She ended the call, pressed the gas harder, and sped toward what she hoped would be one of many forthcoming answers.

CHAPTER SIXTEEN

When she arrived on the third floor, it just so happened that Ellington and Penbrook were walking by the elevators, headed somewhere further down the hallway. When Ellington saw her, he gave Penbrook his apologies and turned back toward her. By the time he had done this, she was already headed for the conference room at the end of the hall.

He hurried to catch up to her. When he was by her side and keeping stride with her, he chuckled. "You're moving fast. I take it you have something?"

"Maybe. You remember the business card on my windshield?"

"Yeah."

"It was a fake. Someone back in DC was screwing with me."

"What?"

She caught him up as they made their way into the vacant conference room. As she came to the end of it, telling him about Harrison's call ten minutes ago, he worked quickly to sync her phone to the laptop and projector on the table. It made her happy to realize that even with a little tension between them they worked fluidly together—both during and after work hours. She hadn't even told him what she had planned to do with the projector and the live-stream, but he had just *known*.

With the projector up and running and the conference room door locked, Mackenzie made the FaceTime call. Harrison answered it right away. It did Mackenzie a bit of good to see the excitement in his face.

"You good to go?" he asked.

"Yeah. Ellington is here, too."

"Okay. There will be a little blip while I connect you to the interrogation room. But just hang on a second."

Harrison put the phone down, pressed a button, and the blip made the screen appear to vibrate. Then, two seconds later, she saw the interrogation room. Agent Yardley was sitting at the table in the center of the room. Across from her was a face she had seen several times but didn't know well. It was a Hispanic male, about her age. He had close-cropped hair and looked to be very nervous.

A voice spoke out from the back of the room. Mackenzie was pretty sure it was McGrath, standing just out of the camera's frame. He was telling her that they were good to go, indicating that Mackenzie was now on the feed.

"Agent Fernandez, you've been a field agent for how long now?" Yardley asked.

"Three months," the man said.

"So when you came into the academy, Agent Mackenzie White was not in your recruitment class, is that correct?"

"That's right."

"But you knew who she was?"

"Yeah, most of us did. She was like this story we were told…an example of how even someone just starting out could rise quickly."

"And had you followed her career at all?"

"Not really. She just has this reputation for being a badass. I'd heard about some cases she wrapped, but I was only interested because she was so young. Hearing those stories *is* a great source of motivation for anyone in the academy."

"Of course. But that's because she worked her ass off," Yardley said. "That, and she's good at what she does."

Yardley leaned back and looked toward McGrath, still off-screen. She was apparently seeing if he wanted to add anything. Apparently, he did not.

"You know why you're here, correct?" Yardley asked Fernandez.

"I am. And I'm sorry—"

"I don't want apologies," Yardley said. "I want to know how you even knew about the card in the first place. How did you know about the Barker Antiques business cards?"

"Someone else told me about them."

"Who?"

"I don't remember. Honestly. There were a bunch of us drinking one night, out at a bar. Someone was talking about this case out in Nebraska that might be linked to the murder of White's father. I found it interesting."

"The murder?"

"No. The case. Like why it reached so far back. So I asked what else they knew."

"And they knew about the business cards?"

Fernandez nodded. While Mackenzie found it irritating that her past had been discussed and dissected by members of the academy at a bar, she also knew that there was no real harm in it. Besides, the

80

bigger details of the case weren't even classified. Anyone without a moral compass and a penchant for digging up dirt within the bureau could have figured it out. And apparently, they had.

"Yeah. They said the killer was leaving behind business cards at the scene. Said there might have even been one there when White's father was murdered."

"And who was telling you all of this?" McGrath asked, his voice coming like some invisible deity from off-screen.

Fernandez looked away, finding his hands suddenly interesting. Mackenzie felt confident that he would not give up a name. There was a sense of camaraderie among those in the academy that, from time to time, rivaled that of men in the military. Oddly, she respected him for it. She knew that despite the lack of cooperation, McGrath would appreciate it, too.

"So why the prank?" Yardley asked.

"Jealousy," Fernandez said. "Word gets around, you know? Sure, we were all sort of looking to White as a beacon almost…*hey, this can happen to you, too.* That sort of thing. But it was also pretty apparent that she'd been primed and hand-picked for her quick rise from the start."

"How so?" Yardley asked.

Fernandez shrugged. "She was teamed up with Agent Ellington. People started seeing her going up to Director McGrath's office. It was…God, it sounds so juvenile but it didn't seem fair. And it didn't take long for this person we looked up to, to become this symbol of how sometimes people just get ahead because of their situation."

"You mean to tell me," McGrath said, "that you thought the case involving her father somehow gave her privilege in the cases and partners she was assigned to?"

"I know now that it wasn't the case. But it seemed that way. The business card…we had a few made up. We thought it would be funny."

"White's father is *dead*," Yardley said. "Do you get that? How in the hell do you think a prank along those lines is funny?"

Mackenzie felt a rush of anger swirling through her. Before she could let it get the best of her she ended the FaceTime call. She then used her phone to text Harrison. **They can do whatever they want with him,** she texted. **But I won't be pressing charges.**

"You didn't want to hear the rest?" Ellington asked.

"No. I heard enough, and I know how it's going to end."

"You okay?"

She nodded, leaning against the wall with her arms crossed. "I'm better than I should be. In the past day or so, I've had to face my mother, found out that I was pranked with the business card in DC, and now I also think I need to go see my sister."

"About the case…or personal?"

"Both."

"Want me to come with you?" Ellington asked. But he asked in a way that made her think he already knew what her answer would be—and it disappointed him.

"No thanks. She's just in Kansas City. If I leave now, I can be back by midnight or so. If things go well."

"Mac…look, I don't know what's going on with you—with *us*—but…"

"Me neither. And now is not the time to figure it out. Do you mind hanging back here while I check in with my sister?"

"Is there even a lead worth looking into?"

She shot him an annoyed look but figured she did owe him an update. So she spent the next five minutes filling him in on her late lunch with Peterson. It was clear that he did not like that she'd met with him, but he said nothing. In the end, he seemed much more excited about the possible connection than the lunch itself.

"And after all that, you still don't want me to go with you? At the risk of pulling rank, this *is* my case, too."

"If it was anyone other than my sister, then it wouldn't even be a question. But you don't understand how it is between the two of us. If I go in as an agent with a partner at my side, she'll be useless. If it's just me, I'll at least stand some sort of chance."

He nodded, resigning himself to the fact that she was right. But that did not mean that he was happy about it.

"Fine," he said. He then headed for the door and Mackenzie couldn't remember a time when she had seen him so pissed off. "Just be sure to fill me in on the details when you have the time."

He left the room before Mackenzie could even try to get another word out. And that was fine with her…because she had nothing to say anyway. She remained leaning against the wall, arms crossed in a defensive posture.

Even when she removed herself from the wall and sat down at the conference room table, she felt rigid and tense, still in a defensive posture. It came from the fact that she knew she'd have to talk to her sister. To that end, she pulled her phone back out, pulled up Stephanie's number for the first time in over a year, and stared at it for a while before finally acting.

CHAPTER SEVENTEEN

Before making her decision to contact Stephanie before simply driving out to Kansas City, Mackenzie decided on two things. One: she would FaceTime her; despite her pig-headedness, she knew that Stephanie was an emotional mess at heart and seeing her sister's face on the other end of a screen might make communicating with her a little easier. Two: she was not going to tell Stephanie that she was in Nebraska. That would only make matters stranger and set Stephanie's internal alarms off.

She placed the FaceTime call and when the line started ringing, Mackenzie didn't even try to pretend that she wasn't nervous as hell. After several seconds, she was sure that Stephanie wouldn't answer her call. But just as she was expecting the ringing to stop, Stephanie answered.

Neither of them spoke right away. They simply stared at one another for the first three seconds, their eyes getting reacquainted with one another. It took Mackenzie to break the silence, and in a very juvenile way it made her feel as if she was instantly on the losing end of the argument.

"Hey, Steph," she said. "Did I catch you at a bad time?"

"Um, not really. I need to get out of here soon to head out to work. What's up?"

"Look, I don't even know how to ease into this, so I'm just going to jump right in. Have you had any sort of relationship with a guy named Trevor Black?"

Right away, any hope of a meaningful conversation went out the window. Mackenzie could see it in Stephanie's eyes. She had gone from surprised and curious to annoyed in less than a second.

"Have you been talking to that detective?" Stephanie asked. "Peters or Peterson or something?"

"Yes, I have. And when he called you, did you listen to him?"

"No. When he said he was calling about a case linked to Dad's death, I refused to speak to him."

"Why?" Mackenzie asked, fully prepared to take part in a full-on argument if it came to that.

"The same reason I never wanted to get into it with you. Because it's in the past and no amount of digging up old stories and facts will bring him back. And it won't fix things between you and me or either of us and Mom, either."

"That's true," Mackenzie said. "But that's an extremely selfish position to take. There are other people being killed, Stephanie. Maybe by the same man that killed Dad. And if—"

"You know what would be great?" Stephanie said. "It would be great if just once, you'd call to say hello. Just to catch up. That's the only reason I answered this call. I thought to myself: *Surely she isn't calling about the case again after the way the last conversation about it went down.* But you proved me wrong right away."

"My apologies," Mackenzie snapped. "Let me start over. How have you been, Steph?"

"I was great until my rude bitch of a sister called me up about two minutes ago," Stephanie said.

And then she hung up.

Out of spite, Mackenzie nearly called her right back. But she allowed herself a few moments to cool down before finally standing up from the table and calmly leaving the room. She did not hesitate or even stop to think as she headed back toward the elevators. She texted Harrison yet again with another request.

I need the address of the workplace of Stephanie White. Somewhere in Kansas City.

Harrison responded back that he'd hop right on it. And with that assurance tucked away, Mackenzie headed out to her car and was pointed in the direction of Kansas City within five minutes.

***

Harrison called her back forty minutes later, while she was well into her nearly three-hour drive to Kansas City. Evening was slowly giving way to night, casting an eerie sort of dark orange glow to the highway. It was mesmerizing and, in a strange way, calming. It was exactly what she needed to gear herself up for the confrontation to come.

"What have you got for me?" Mackenzie asked.

"Well, it was harder than I thought. And, well…maybe a little awkward. Her last reported place of employment was a small shipping plant for a retail chain. But there are no records of her working there for more than sixteen months. However, I dug a bit more and saw that she was listed as a witness to a lethal bar brawl at a strip club. In the report, she's listed as being an employee there."

Yes…sounds about right, Mackenzie thought. "Dare I ask what this place is called?"

"Pinky's Dream."

"My God," she sighed. "Thanks, Harrison."

She then typed in the poorly chosen name of Pinky's Dream into her GPS and set her phone down again. She headed east, aware that the last two days had been nothing more than traveling, constant motion moving toward…where? She wasn't even sure. She was starting to feel like she was running in circles, somehow always coming back to this one case—to this one point in her life that had been clutching at her from an early age.

But maybe, just maybe, she was coming to the end of it. Something about visiting her mother and currently on the trail of her sister made her feel like she was coming full circle.

The question, though, was how her life might change when that circle came to a close.

***

Night had fully fallen by the time Mackenzie pulled her car into the lot of Pinky's Dream. It wasn't even nine o'clock yet and being a Wednesday night, the lot was pretty much empty. As she got out of the car, it occurred to her that by walking inside, there was a very good chance that she'd have to see Stephanie in the midst of an act. It only made her anxiety worse, causing her stomach to tremble to the point where she thought she might actually be sick.

When she walked in, it also occurred to her that she had never been in a strip club. However, the depictions she had seen in movies were pretty accurate. Dim lighting everywhere other than on the stage, which was adorned in flashing blue and white lights. Three women were currently on stage in various stages of undress, one swinging around a pole while the other two danced suggestively together.

One of the dancers was Stephanie. She was playing the part well, writhing against the other woman in a way that Mackenzie found almost comical but in a way she also knew would appeal to just about any male with a pulse. The music over the PA was unfamiliar to her but had a sort of groove-infused industrial feel straight out of the early nineties.

Not knowing what else to do, Mackenzie walked to the right-hand side of the place and got a seat at the bar. It, too, was pretty dead. The handful of patrons were out near the stage. A few were sitting in darker corners, getting private dances.

"Can I get you a drink?" the bartender asked.

"God yes," she said. "Rum and Coke, but not too strong."

The bartender went off about his business and as Mackenzie did her best to look at anything other than the stage, she hoped that Stephanie would be free after the song ended.

The bartender came back with her drink and she downed nearly half of it in one swallow. He gave her an amused look before turning his attention to a customer at the other end of the bar. With the song still going, Mackenzie couldn't help herself. She turned her attention back to her sister. Stephanie had always been gorgeous—by far the prettier of them. She'd also been crazy smart but had ended up with the wrong crowd and making some bad decisions: a pregnancy that ended up in a miscarriage at seventeen, a few misdemeanors before she was eighteen, and, of course, her current occupation.

She was also a very good actress, apparently. She legitimately seemed to enjoy what she was doing onstage. The fact that her breasts were bare and her midsection was covered by the thinnest of G-strings apparently did not bother her. Her blonde hair caught the lights and her body moved in sync with the music.

Maybe she is *happy with this life,* Mackenzie thought. *Meanwhile, I'm a bit of a wreck. So who the hell am I to judge?*

The song came to a close and Mackenzie was glad to see that the three women on stage were indeed taking their leave. As they made their exit, though, a few men sitting by the stage came closer and offered a few dollars, shoving them into the lacy bands of the underwear of the three women. She watched as Stephanie lovingly ran one of her hands along one of the men's arm, her smile looking to be genuine.

As Stephanie and the other dancers came down off of the stage, Mackenzie saw that they were heading toward the bar. One of them stopped at the other end of the bar to flirt with the man sitting there. The other two approached the bartender. Mackenzie watched as Stephanie took a bottled water from him. As she took a sip from it, she took a look around the place, maybe trying to eye her next target.

When she saw Mackenzie sitting there, she nearly dropped the water. And for just a fleeting moment, Mackenzie saw a smile on her sister's face. Maybe it was from shock, or maybe surprise. Whatever the cause, it looked quite real.

Slowly, Stephanie came walking over to her. Even then she did not seem uncomfortable that her body was exposed. As she closed the distance between them, Stephanie shrugged and said: "Like the outfit?"

"I do. I don't think it comes in my size, though."

Stephanie laughed at this and took another sip of her water. "What the hell are you doing here?" she asked. "I thought I made it clear—"

"Yeah, well, I was already sort of in the neighborhood. I was at the FBI field office in Omaha."

"You can't stay away from it, can you?" Stephanie asked.

Almost ashamed, Mackenzie shook her head. "I'm close, Stephanie. I've already had to talk to Mom."

"Holy shit. How is she?" "She says she's fine. She's just...I don't know. Just *existing*, I guess. Look...all I need is about ten or fifteen minutes of your time. If I have to, I'll hang out until you clock out."

Stephanie sighed and looked around the place. "No need for that," she said with a frown. "It's pretty dead right now. It'll pick up around ten. I can give you some time."

"Can we talk somewhere other than this?"

"Sure." Stephanie leaned over the bar and whistled. "Hey, Gary! This is my sister. I'm paying for her drink and I'm also heading upstairs to talk with her for a bit. I'll be back in fifteen minutes."

"Your sister?" the bartender asked. "I don't guess she's looking for a job, is she?"

Stephanie shook her head and laughed. "No. She's got bigger and better plans."

"Go on up, then," he said. "But make it quick."

"You heard the man," Stephanie said. "Come on."

Stephanie led her away from the bar. It was a surreal moment—not only seeing her sister but being led through a strip club. Stephanie led her to the back of the larger room where a Duran Duran song had come on for a new batch of dancers. Stephanie opened a door at the back edge of the room and led Mackenzie up a small set of stairs. At the top, she opened another door and led her into what Mackenzie assumed was some sort of changing area. Several mirrors and vanities were set up along a brick wall, all adorned with bright fluorescent lights overhead. On a rack in the back, an assortment of skanky outfits hung from hooks.

"You know, I should be pissed at you," Stephanie said. "I basically told you to leave me alone."

"You did. And I wanted to," Mackenzie admitted. "But the case has gotten to the point where I have to see you as just another potential lead—a source of information. I have to stay professional and not see you as my sister. So when a potential lead gets shitty with me on the phone and refuses to help, I end up coming to see them face-to-face."

"Okay then…Trevor Black. What do you need to know?"

"Were you dating him?" Mackenzie asked.

"For a while. It was just sex at first. Things got a little serious…sleeping over and actual dinner dates, things like that. We both saw where it was going, didn't like it, and bailed."

"What do you know about him? What did he do for work?"

"I don't know that I can say."

"I hate to ask…but you know he's dead, right?"

"Yes. One of those fires out in California. But still…if you go digging on him, you could end up after some of his friends."

"I don't care," Mackenzie said. "Do you have any ties to friends of his that might have less than stellar records?"

"Nothing beyond just knowing them."

"Fine then. You shouldn't care either. Here's where I am right now."

She then revealed to her everything Peterson had told her—about the strange connection Trevor Black had with one of the recently killed vagrants. Stephanie seemed legitimately shocked by the revelation and Mackenzie could see her piecing it together in her mind.

"You think it was just a messed up coincidence?" Stephanie asked.

"If my job has taught me anything, it's that even coincidences need to be fully investigated. But being that Trevor is dead makes it hard to really look into it. So that's why I'm here. I need to know if he might have been involved in anything that could have linked him to a killer that seems currently obsessed with killing homeless people…yet also likely had a hand in killing our father."

Stephanie sighed as she pulled a robe from the rack in the back, finally covering herself up. "When he and I were dating, he was doing some sort of auto parts trading and selling thing online. A small business sort of thing. Nothing illegal as far as I know. But I do know that he has a pretty rough history. Some drug charges and a breaking and entering from his younger days."

"But you don't know any specifics?"

"No. And I see the way you're looking at me. Yeah, he wasn't a stand-up guy. He was a fuck-up, if we're being honest. But we had fun and he never mistreated me."

"I didn't look at you any way."

"Yes, you did. You looked like you're afraid you might burst into flames at any moment since I saw you at the bar. I'm sorry if this setting makes you uncomfortable. I'm sorry if you're more comfortable in the gridlock and cesspool of DC."

"Why are you getting so defensive? I'm sorry that I had to question you about some loser you slept with. But that's where the trail led me."

"Well, just follow the trail back to Omaha because it stops here," Stephanie said. "God...why can't you let this go?"

"It's sort of my job to *not* let it go, Steph."

"Way to use your job as an excuse. Well, what about in high school and college? You were always so hung up on it. Guilt-ridden just like Mom. Well, unlike the two of you, I refuse to let some very bad event from a night almost twenty years ago ruin my life."

And that's what did it. That's what snapped something inside of Mackenzie. She felt something venomous rising to the surface as she strode across the room and got into Stephanie's face.

"You don't think it's affected your life? You're so damn scared to move too far away from home. Why do you think that is? It's because you're tied to the place. It's because it's haunting you, too. You just choose not to face it!"

"And you think strapping on a badge and a gun makes you some superhero? How long have you been wrestling with it, Mackenzie? How long? And look what it's gotten you! You're bitter and torn up and a failure! All these years chasing it down and what do you have to show for it? Nothing!"

Mackenzie caught herself at the last minute, restraining herself from punching her sister. "At least I'm trying," she said. "I committed myself to something. What have you done other than bury yourself in a series of loser men, drinking, stripping for men who go home and do God knows what..."

"You holier-than-thou bitch! Do you have any idea how much money I make here in a month? I guarantee you it's more than you're getting out of that government paycheck. Keep judging, Mackenzie. It just shows how very fucking little you know about me."

Mackenzie knew that she was going to have to leave or else this was going to get bad. She could get into some serious trouble for striking her sister. And she also didn't want to cost Stephanie her job.

So, with those facts in mind, she stepped away and turned her back on her sister. "Thanks for your time, Stephanie. I'll leave now and—"

She stopped herself from making another barbed comment, wanting to end it with *so you can head back down and show your ass to men you've never met.* But fortunately, she was just rational-minded enough to take the high road. It was alarming how easy it had been to resort to insults and screaming when in Stephanie's presence.

"Yeah, thanks for stopping by," Stephanie called out. "Be sure you call me again in another year when you still haven't gotten anywhere on this case!"

Mackenzie kept walking, heading out of the changing room and down the flight of stairs. When she went back out into the main area, the stage was now lit in a pulsing red light. A single dancer was at work on the stage, swaying and gyrating to a techno rhythm. She hurried out, casting her eyes to the floor, and did not look up until she was back out into the parking lot.

As she passed by a plastic display for the night's beer specials just outside the door, she couldn't resist. She pulled her arm back and punched it as hard as she could. The plastic cracked and the sign went to the pavement in a satisfying clatter. By the time she got to her car, she realized that three of her knuckles were bleeding.

She didn't care. In that moment, she actually enjoyed the sting.

She headed back to Omaha, upset that she had nothing new to contribute to the case but thankful that the meeting with Stephanie was over. While that full-circle sensation did not yet feel closed, she could at least appreciate the curvature of it and sense the end of it just ahead.

CHAPTER EIGHTEEN

When she got back to the motel in Omaha, it was 12:11 in the morning. She unlocked the door quietly, expecting Ellington to be asleep. However, when she stepped inside, she found him standing by the small table by the bed, typing something into his laptop. He was still dressed in his suit pants but had lost the button-up shirt, wearing just the tank top he wore beneath it. It was cute and comforting somehow and she found herself wanting to just collapse into his arms.

But there was no way she was going to be vulnerable with him after the last few days they'd had—especially not after the hectic encounter she recently had with her sister. So as she walked into the room, she offered him a simple "Hey," and nothing else.

"Hey yourself," he said. "How did it go?"

"As I'd expected. But I do feel pretty confident that she doesn't know anything about Trevor Black. She seemed shocked when I told her."

"Anything else?"

"A screaming match that I'd really rather not get into."

She walked straight into the restroom, relieved herself, and then started to strip down for a shower. She half expected Ellington to join her—and she wanted him to, honestly. But she knew it would mean very little; it would just be furthering their routine. Which made her wonder, not for the first time, exactly what they were to one another. Was it just sex? Was it just the fact that they worked together and knew one another well?

He ended up not joining her and when she dried off, she made sure the door stayed closed. It was almost a game of sorts; if they were still upset with one another, she was not going to allow him to see her naked...which was ridiculous when she thought about it.

Wrapped in a towel, she headed back out into the room and grabbed clothes. She returned to the bathroom to change and when she came back out, Ellington was shutting down his computer. They both looked awkwardly at the single bed and it was almost as if the sight of it presented them with the opportunity to finally talk about what was going on.

As he usually did, Ellington started. When any conversation took a turn toward what their relationship was, he was usually the one to kick it off.

"So what's the deal?" he asked. "I care a great deal about you and I want to be there for you…but these last two days, I just can't tell what it is you need."

"That's because I don't know what I need myself. This thing with meeting my mom and my sister…it was unexpected, but at the same time, I felt like I knew it was coming. Like I had to do it sooner or later. The fact that the meetings were both related to this damned case just made it even more confusing."

"I get that," he said. "But I'd like to think you'd know by now that you can rely on me for anything like that. With work or your personal life. I understand that you don't particularly like to talk about your family but if you and I are ever going to grow, I think you *have* to let me in on some if it."

"I don't *have* to do anything of the sort," she said, hating the way it sounded when it came out of her mouth.

"Well, I can't keep just dancing around things like I have these last few days when the topic of your dad's case or your family pops up."

"I don't know what to tell you," she said, very much aware that some of the venom from her meeting with Stephanie was still swarming within her. "Maybe if you want us to work out in the end, you should ask McGrath to take you off the case."

"No," Ellington said. He didn't snap the response out, but it still sounded pretty hostile. "If anyone needs to be pulled from the case, it's you. Mac…you're *way* too close to this. And driving back and forth and back and forth to have these meetings with your mom and sister…it's counterproductive. You're making it much harder on yourself than it has to be."

"And how the fuck would you know how hard it is on me?" she said, nearly yelling at him.

"Because I know you well enough to know when you aren't thinking clearly. That's how. Whether you like it or not, I know you, Mac. And it's more than just work, more than just sex. I know you and I love you and this is just too hard."

"Too hard? Which part?"

He sat on the bed, looking away from her. "The being in love with you part. Because honestly, I don't have the energy to invest myself in it if you're going to push me away."

She thought very briefly about the feeling that had come across her when she'd come into the room and saw him working on his

92

laptop—the need for him to hold her, her need to crumple up against him. What if he knew about those things? What if he knew that whenever she felt broken, he was the first person she wanted to go to?

But there was no way she could tell him those things now. *He just told you he loves you,* she told herself. *You open up right now and things are going to get messy...*

"I'm not pushing you away," she said.

"It feels like it," he said. "And you know...with this case, maybe that's okay. Maybe that's for the best. And maybe we can make it easier."

"How?" she asked.

"By calling it a night and going to bed. I can get another room if you want. Maybe if I'm out of the equation, this whole mess will be easier for you. So from this point on, I'm nothing more than your partner. And if tomorrow goes like today and yesterday did, then yeah...I'll call McGrath and ask him to take me off the case. But then he'll ask why. And do you really want to open that can of worms? He'll take you off of it before he'll take me off."

"Ellington, I—"

"You figure it out," he said. "I'm going to sleep...unless you need me to get another room."

"No...don't be stupid."

Sliding under the covers, his back still to her, he said: "Good night, Mac."

She didn't say a word. She almost *did* want him to be in another room because she hated the way she was acting toward him.

Mackenzie slowly sat down on the edge of the bed. She looked at the little red marks on her knuckles from where she'd punched the display sign outside of Pinky's Dream and frowned. She then looked at the reflection of herself in the mirror of the little dresser across the room. She stared herself down and a single, very direct thought went through her head.

You'd better wrap this case up, she thought. *Because maybe Stephanie is right. Maybe it is ruining your life. And it will continue to do so until the circle closes.*

***

Sleep was surprisingly easy to find once she got into bed and killed the lights. It helped tremendously that she finally allowed herself a moment to break down under the covers and in the darkness. She sobbed quietly into her pillow when she knew for

93

sure Ellington was asleep. She knew that one powerful breakdown might just help to relieve some tension and stress.

She cried harder than she could remember crying anytime since middle school and, quite honestly, wasn't all that ashamed of it. She cried for the state of the lives of her mother and sister. She cried because she felt she was basically sabotaging things with Ellington. She cried because, despite the fact that she had seen more of her family members in the last thirty-six hours than she had in the last year of her life, she had never felt more alone in her life.

It was the sobbing that helped her get to sleep so easily. It may have also been why her saddened and tired mind was so susceptible to the nightmares again.

In the nightmare, she found herself standing in the vacant lot behind the Super Saver grocery store where the last vagrant had been killed. She was there by herself, looking to the back wall of the abandoned store. All along the ground, there were the bodies of homeless people. There were so many of them that their blood was literally running along the pavement. The soles of Mackenzie's feet were sticky with it.

As she walked closer to the bodies, she saw several business cards riding the thick tide of blood toward her. Every single one carried the print of Barker Antiques. She kicked at a few of them on her way to the bodies, the air thick with a copper-like smell as she splattered more and more blood up onto her shoes.

"Hey, hold on," someone called from behind her.

She turned and saw her father standing at the back of the alley. Stephanie was with him, scantily clad as if she were about to hit the stage at work. She looked like she had been crying.

"Dad?"

"They're dead," he said simply. "No point in looking for survivors. Just look at all of the blood."

"But I don't know where else to look."

He shrugged. "The past, maybe. We can't look to the future for answers…not even the present most of the time. Just the past."

"But the past…looking there makes me feel like a failure," she said.

"Nonsense. Look how far you've come."

"Dad…"

"Nope. I won't hear it. You hurry now. And watch out behind you."

Confused, she turned around toward the bodies again. There was a new body there, standing up and walking toward her. It was covered in blood from head to toe.

It was Ellington, reaching out to her with hands soaked in maroon. He was whimpering and when he opened his mouth to speak to her, there was blood there as well.

"Help," he said. "Together...me and you...we can help. But you have to help me first..."

She reached out to him and his whimpers became a thick, guttural laugh. The blood that was lodged in his mouth and throat came out in one big splatter that struck her in the face. And even as she stumbled backward and fell into the still-running pool of blood, Ellington laughed and laughed and—

Mackenzie shot up in bed, her arms reaching like phantoms toward an Ellington that was not there. Confused and blurry-eyed, she finally realized that it had just been a dream—a very vivid dream.

Not only that, but her cell phone was ringing. It was the noise that had yanked her so violently out of her nightmare.

She fumbled for it in the darkness with one hand while clicking on the bedside lamp with her other. She didn't even bother checking the display. She was so disoriented that she answered it blindly.

"This is White," she said.

"Mackenzie?"

It was Stephanie's voice. The last voice she'd expected to hear anytime soon, if ever again.

"Yeah? Hey, Steph. What is it?"

"I um...shit."

Mackenzie looked to the bedside clock and saw that it was 2:25. None of this made sense to her as she still tried to properly wake herself up. She was both scared and hopeful at the same time. Ellington had roused from sleep and was turning toward her. She quickly got out of bed and closed herself in the bathroom to continue the call.

"I'm sorry, Mac," Stephanie said as Mackenzie closed the bathroom door. "I'm sorry. You're right. What happened to Dad *has* haunted me. I've never dealt with it because I don't know how. And it's not fair of me to attack you for that or for the fact that you've done something with your life."

"It's okay, Steph. I said some messed up things, too."

"Yeah...but...ugh."

The tone of Stephanie's voice made Mackenzie think her sister had been drinking. It made sense; it would explain the courage it had taken to call at such an hour so soon after their confrontation.

"Anyway," Stephanie said. "I was telling the truth about Trevor. I don't think he was really into anything bad when I knew

95

him. But as the night went on, these questions kept popping up in my head. Recommendations I wanted to give to you."

"Like what?"

"Like Amy Lucas. Do you remember her? Have you spoken with her about any of this?"

"I have, actually. It went nowhere. Well…maybe not nowhere. She did mention something about Dad I never knew. Did you know he dabbled in real estate before we were born? Just some random apartment building, apparently."

Stephanie chuckled. "No. But God, that's hilarious. I can't see it."

"Me neither."

"You know, Trevor had some sort of thing going on with housing. Maybe with HUD? I don't even remember."

"Like as a job?" Mackenzie asked.

"I don't know. I hate to admit it, but it was just sex. When he talked, I barely listened. I'm sorry."

"No, it's fine. Any other recommendations?"

"Yeah. You know that group Dad used to sometimes hang with on the weekends? Some sort of men's club down at the Legion Hall."

"Oh yeah! God. I'd almost forgotten. They played darts and poker or something like that? Watched football every now and then on Sundays."

"Yeah. I only remember them because one of their sons was the first guy I ever kissed. I thought about him the other day, actually."

"Do you remember the dad's name?" Mackenzie asked.

"No. Sorry. Shit…I'm not helping at all, am I?"

Another possible real estate link. Another whole group of people that can maybe tell me about Dad?

"Actually, that's a lot of help. Thanks."

"Sure. And Mac…I mean it. I'm sorry."

"It's okay."

"Then prove it," Stephanie said. "When you wrap this case up, give me a call. Let's catch up…only after this is all behind us. Sound good?"

"I've love that. Take care, Steph. And thanks for calling."

Following the call, she took a moment to collect her thoughts and allow herself to fully wake up—a hard task after getting only two hours of sleep. She wanted to get in her car and head back to Belton right away. But on just two hours of sleep, she knew that it would be hazardous. Instead, she relied on Harrison once again, shooting him an email on her phone rather than a text due to the late hour.

I need you to look into a recently deceased guy named Trevor Black, she typed. *He died recently in the California wildfire out near Napa. Has a record but I'm more interested in whatever history he has involving real estate or low income housing. Not an urgent matter, but the sooner I can get the info, the better.*

With the email sent, she walked back out into the room. Ellington was sitting up now, gazing at her with a look of anticipation. "Your sister?" he asked.

"Yeah. She…she apologized for the way things went." She left it at that, not telling him about the potential lead.

And why not? a tiny voice in the back of her head asked.

"That's it?" he asked.

"Yeah," she said, slipping back into bed and turning her back to him.

She felt Ellington settling in as well, and wondered if he'd snuggle up behind her. After five minutes when she heard his light snoring, she got her answer. This time, in the darkness and with her conversation with Stephanie in her head, it was much harder to go to sleep. Her mind kept dragging up memories of Belton and her father leaving on Sunday afternoons to hang with some friends she had never met to watch a football game down at the Legion Hall.

As the memories came, as vague as they were, sleep became more elusive. She finally did drift back off around 3:30 but even then, it was a thin sleep that evaporated completely when the first light of day crept through the blinds at 6:55. It took her a moment to realize that it was the sound of the door closing that had stirred her awake.

She looked to her left and saw that Ellington was gone. There was a slip of paper on the bed, a note written in his handwriting.

Walked down to the lobby for coffee and muffins. Be right back.

She wasted no time. She got out of bed, got dressed, and brushed her teeth. She picked up her phone and sent Ellington a brief message. **Going back to Belton. Will let you know if I'll be any later than tomorrow morning getting back.**

She felt like she was a teenager, running away. She wanted to run to the lobby and ask him to go with her. But she had to do this alone…or so she thought.

She kept checking her phone, expecting it to ding, expecting to see the familiar and secure sight of Ellington's name pop up.

But Ellington did not respond.

And honestly, Mackenzie didn't blame him.

CHAPTER NINETEEN

She went directly to the Legion Hall, which was located on the western edge of Belton. It sat off of the highway, situated in the midst of a paved parking lot that was in desperate need of repair. When she parked in the lot at 2:05, she only saw five cars in the parking lot—one of them apparently belonging to the man she saw sitting on a riding lawn mower, making a lap around the back lawn.

She allowed herself a moment to stretch her back before entering. The driving and tension of the last two days had caught up to her. Every muscle felt tight, every joint inflamed and sore. She knew she couldn't keep journeying back and forth whenever it pleased her. Not only was it a good way to slow down the progress of the case, but it was also taking its toll on her.

When she walked into Legion Hall, it wasn't at all the sort of place she had been expecting. Quite honestly, it looked like little more than a common room within a retirement home—maybe a bit better decorated. A television sat against the far wall, currently tuned to a game show that had been turned down to a murmur. She imagined her father sitting in front of it with several other men, bickering about football, and it brought a smile to her face.

There were three people in the room. One elderly lady was knitting something while sitting on a large couch. From time to time, she'd glance up at the game show while her fingers worked on muscle memory at the project in her lap. On the far side of the room, two men were playing a card game. One of the men looked older—perhaps seventy or so—while the other was surely no older than fifty.

Playing the odds, she walked over to the two men. The older man was facing her and when he saw her approaching, he gave her a peculiar look.

"You lost, sweetie?" he asked. There was grit in his voice, yet when he called her *sweetie*, she took no offense to it.

"No, I don't believe I am," she said. She then showed the men her ID and introduced herself, giving her name as quickly as possible in the hope these men would not get hung up on her last name. In Belton, she knew it would be a risk wherever she went.

"FBI?" the maybe-fifty-year-old said. "In Belton?"

"Yes sir," she said. "I'm trying to gather some information on a murder that occurred in town about twenty years ago. To this day, it's gone unsolved and we believe the killer may be at work again in Omaha."

"And how might we help?" the older gentleman asked, now bored with the card game—a game of rummy, Mackenzie saw now that she was next to the table.

"Could I get your names, first of all?"

The older man seemed suspicious for a moment but then gave in. "Ed Patterson."

"And I'm Bernie Toombs," the fifty-something said.

"Thanks, gentlemen. I wonder if either of you knew a man by the name of Benjamin White. He died about eighteen years ago and—"

Ed Patterson started to chuckle in a way that seemed whimsical, but coming out of his throat, seemed a bit sad.

"Something funny?" Mackenzie asked.

"Hell yeah, I knew Ben. He was a local cop. Good guy, but man did he suck at darts."

"So you knew him personally?" Mackenzie asked.

"I did. He used to hang out here from time to time. We had this informal dart league that run out of the Legion Hall. It usually just turned into a bunch of guys drinking, though. Ben was on my team and man...he was *not* good. Jesus...I haven't thought of Ben in ages."

"And you?" Mackenzie asked the other man.

"I knew who he was," he said. "I saw him in here every now and then, too. I was only thirty or so back then, though. A few years younger than him, I guess. I only ever saw him on Sundays when football was on. And yeah...he seemed like a good guy. He was a Chiefs fan, though...so that was a damn shame."

As quick as a lightning bolt, a memory surfaced in Mackenzie's head. She could see her father toiling around the house or doing yardwork. A ratty old Kansas City Chiefs cap was pulled down over his head, so low that it was hard to see his eyes. She hadn't necessarily forgotten about this detail of her father, but it had been pushed somewhere to the far recesses of her memories. To see it so clearly for the first time in forever was almost overwhelming.

"So, Mr. Patterson, it seems like you knew him enough to think of him as a friend. Would that be safe to say?"

"I suppose. I mean, he was a good twenty or twenty-five years younger than me, but yeah. I guess I did think of him as a friend.

Besides that, I have always had a lot of respect for cops. It's a thankless job most of the time."

"Did he ever mention his family?" she asked.

"Yeah, from time to time. He had two daughters, if I recall. And his wife...the poor woman. I think she sort of went crazy after he died."

Thankful that he had not paid much attention to her name when she had introduced herself, Mackenzie went on before he could make the connection.

"Do you remember if you knew him before he had children?"

Ed thought about this for a while and then gave a slow, hesitant nod. "I think so. Yes, I remember some of us men giving him a good deal of ribbing when he first got married. That's when I first met him...not too long after he got married. I don't know how much longer it was after that before he had kids, though. Maybe a couple of years."

"And do you know anything about his work life before he became a cop, or right when he started being a cop?"

Again, Ed had to take a moment to reach back into his memories. "I don't think so," he finally said. "As far as I know, that's all he ever did."

"Well," Bernie spoke up, "he did dabble in being a landlord for a while. I actually rented one of the apartments he oversaw."

Thank the Lord for small towns, Mackenzie thought.

"You're telling me that you rented a property from Benjamin White when he was running an apartment complex?" Mackenzie asked.

"Yeah. But *property* is being too generous. The place was a hole. He did the best he could with the shitty building he had, but it was too much for him, I think. He ended up getting rid of it. And I moved out not too long after that."

"Yeah, I do remember him grumbling about that," Ed said. A proud smile crossed his face as he firmly grasped on to a previously buried memory.

"And Mr. Toombs, where was this property?"

"Over in Elm Branch," he said. "It's on a street that's basically dried up and dead, but the building is still there. No one's operated it in years, though."

Elm Branch, she thought as her heart kicked up into a whole different gear. She knew Elm Branch well. It was a bit bigger than Belton, located one town over to the east—a car ride of about fifteen minutes.

Her nerves felt like fire and she could not get out of the Legion Hall fast enough. Part of her wanted to revel in the fact that this was a place that had once meant something to her father. But the time for nostalgia was over. What was the point in hanging around her father's old haunts when she finally had a solid connection?

"Do you recall the exact address?" Mackenzie asked Toombs.

"Yeah. It was my first residence so it sort of stuck in my brain—like your first phone number, you know? It was 167 Spruce Street."

"Thank you," she said. "Finally, would you gentleman mind providing me with your phone numbers in case I need any further information?"

In the end, they were both happy to oblige. Ed Patterson in particular seemed quite excited to be a part of it. The resurfaced memories of an old friend had him smiling wider than she had seen since stepping foot into the Legion Hall.

Mackenzie left with both numbers saved into her phone, though she had a feeling that she likely wouldn't use them. She'd come to recognize the moment in a case when things took an upswing—when the countless dead ends had piled up high enough to allow her to see the fruits of a promising lead.

She felt that upswing as she got into her car and headed toward Elm Branch for the first time since she was fourteen years old. She nearly called Stephanie to thank her for the suggestion but decided not to. She was finally moving forward, able to start pushing the past behind her. And until she could successfully do that, she thought it best that all other things from her past stay in the rearview as well.

As she started toward the town of Elm Branch, her phone rang. It was Harrison and he sounded relatively proud of himself.

"Trevor Black," he said. "I got results. He died recently in a wildfire out in Napa. I looked into any dealings he had with real estate, like you asked. It turns out he *was* involved in a small construction project to renovate low-income homes. So sort of a charitable thing he did as a part of his parole."

"Where was this?" she asked.

"Lincoln, Nebraska."

"Any idea how he ended up in Napa?"

"Living with an aunt from what I can see. The aunt made it out of the house before the fire took it. Trevor was not so lucky."

"The charitable construction," she said. "Does it check out?"

"Yeah. I had someone call the organization. They said their records show Trevor Black worked his butt off and never caused any problems. They referred to him as an okay guy that just needed to grow up a bit."

Too late for that now, Mackenzie thought morbidly as she realized that the Trevor Black lead was now a dead end.

"Thanks, Harrison," she said, ending the call.

She drove toward Elm Branch, pushing the dead end away with an image of her father in her mind. His Chiefs cap was pushed down on his head and he was carrying a wrench in his hand, headed out to fix up the old beater car he had kept in the driveway but rarely used.

In the recollection, he was smiling.

Outside of her nightmares, it was the clearest memory she had of him with a genuine smile on his face.

She kept it in the center of her mind as she sped out of Belton and toward another little city where her father had tried to make a name for himself before she had even been a twinkle in his eye.

She felt the circle slowly closing—if not for the case itself, then certainly for this ragged thread of her past.

CHAPTER TWENTY

Bernie Toombs had been right; everything on Spruce Street had gone out of business. Most of the town of Elm Branch had gone the same route. There was a Subway on the corner of Spruce and, a few lots down, a barber shop that appeared to be open. But other than that, the street was dead. And that included the derelict apartment building located at 167.

She parked her car in front of the building and looked up at it. It certainly wasn't any fitting monument to her father but it was still significant in that it had been a part of his life—a part that Mackenzie had not known about until three days ago. Right away, she saw that the front door had been barricaded with a thick set of chains and locks. Several boards had been nailed across the double doors as well. Probably a precaution taken by the town rather than the last owner, hoping to prevent injury from a curious resident.

Mackenzie walked around the building, taking a route down a thin alley between the apartment building and what appeared to have once been a department store. She wasn't sure why, but something about being in the shadows of these two buildings in a city that had basically dried up and died had her hand hovering anxiously over her Glock.

Around back, she came to a small parking lot. Weeds had found cracks to spring up through in most places. Several old green trash cans lay on their sides, glass bottles, plastic trash, and other debris scattered around them. It did not look like a place anyone had frequented in a very long time.

The rear of the building offered a single back door to go through. It, too, had been padlocked. Mackenzie looked around for another way in and found one easily enough. An old rusted ladder from a fire escape hung down, but not within her grasp. Feeling rather like a child, she pulled over one of the green trash bins and stood it up underneath the ladder. Climbing carefully on top of it, she was able to position herself to reach the ladder and pull it down. Flakes of rust rained down as the ladder gave a shriek, its bolts and pulleys having sat dormant for so long.

She climbed the ladder up to the first platform, an iron structure that felt far too flimsy for her comfort. Fortunately, the first window she came to was warped and rotten. It took only a single kick to knock the frame loose. She used the butt of her Glock to knock all of the loose pieces of glass away and then ducked through the place where the window had been.

She found herself in a small gutted apartment. The place smelled of mildew and something rotten—something somewhere between a decomposing animal and long-rotted food. It was a small apartment, equipped with a living area and kitchen that were separated by a thin half-bar, a single bedroom, and a small bathroom. Unless it had been somehow drastically different when her father had given it a go nearly thirty years ago, she was pretty sure he had been defeated before he really even got started.

She left the apartment and found herself in a hallway. It was lit by dusty sunlight that came through the windows on each end. The hallway contained ten different apartments, five on each side. Judging from what she had seen on the outside, the building was four stories tall. Even if the bottom floor was taken up by administrative offices, that was still a lot of apartments for one man to manage.

Assuming there *was* an office of some kind on the first floor (she was currently on the second), Mackenzie found a stairwell at the western end of the hall. As she took them down, she saw the skeleton of what was likely a rat, along with petrified droppings. Dead insects also littered the stairway, but much to her surprise, there was no sign of vandalism or vagrants.

Her hunch had been correct; the first floor contained only two apartments, a public restroom, and a tiny office space. The office was about the size of half of one of the living rooms in the apartments. There was a large but ugly desk still sitting in the office that took up most of the space. It was empty except for the layers of dust blanketing the top. The walls and ceiling were rich with cobwebs and collected dust. Two old filing cabinets sat against the back wall, providing hardly any room between where the desk sat and the cabinets started. She found them locked but they were so old that it took only a little brute force to spring them open.

There was hardly anything in them. Old scraps of paper, a few old pens, more dust and dirt. However, in the bottom drawer of the second one, she found an old invoice. It was from twenty-nine years ago, a payment made to a painting company. Her hands trembled a bit when she saw the signature at the bottom of the page.

Benjamin White.

She set it down with care on the dusty desk and stared at it. She didn't necessarily feel like she had been lied to, but she couldn't help but wonder what other things she had not known about her father. Sure, a failed gig as a landlord was nothing to brag to your kids about, but still…she couldn't get over the feeling of being cheated.

She checked the drawers on the old desk and found nothing but a few empty file folders and scattered paper clips. She shut the last one gingerly, a little disappointed that this was all the building had to offer. She leaned against the desk, looking around the place and imagining seeing her father in the same space, only much cleaner.

The dust seemed to almost glow from the afternoon sunlight that spilled into the office through the one large window in the back of the room. She looked out the window and saw Jefferson Street, which ran parallel to Spruce. Jefferson was also mostly dead, the four buildings she could clearly see all closed and shuttered.

She turned and looked away, ready to leave, when she saw something out of the corner of her eye.

No, she thought. *No way. You're seeing things…*

But she knew this wasn't true. Slowly, she turned back toward the window and stepped closer to it. She looked across the street. She stared at the four buildings. Two were featureless and there was no indication of what they had once been. The third still had the letters in the window, proclaiming the name of the failed business as Elm Branch Jewelers. Directly beside it, connected without even the break of an alleyway, was a shop with a faded and torn awning over the door.

The tear in the awning had removed a portion of the business name, but enough of it remained to make a very educated guess.

Mackenzie's heart felt like it stopped beating for about five seconds as she looked at the awning and the incomplete name of the business.

RKER ANTIQUES

When her heart felt like it had started to beat again, Mackenzie drew in a deep breath and ran out of the office her father had once attempted to do business in.

***

Outside, she took a deep inhale of the fresh air, glad to be out of the dusty sour smell of the apartment building. She ran across the street, not bothering to look for traffic because there was none. She looked at the awning again just to make sure her eyes weren't playing tricks on her.

She still saw the same letters. The tear in the awning followed by RKER ANTIQUES. She approached the building and stepped under the awning. There were no vinyl letters on the window or doors, but she could clearly see where they had once been. The ghosts of those letters were on the glass of the door, the adhesive to the letters stubbornly clinging to it.

PARKER ANTIQUES.

It was too funny—so funny that she found herself reading it out loud. "Parker Antiques," she said, testing the words.

It's not Barker *Antiques,* she thought, *but it's damned close. Could be another of those coincidences that keep popping up.*

But this one was too close to home. Something about this one pulled at her heart and her logic. This coincidence could not be ignored. As she stared at the filmy remnants of those letters on the door, she pulled out her phone. Rather than send a text, she took the time to actually call Harrison this time.

"Hey, White," he answered after the third ring. "What can I do for you?"

"I need you to find the current name and address of anyone who owned a business in Elm Branch, Nebraska, called Parker Antiques."

"You said *Parker*?"

"Yeah, that's right. And if you could expedite this one somehow, that would be great."

"I'll see what I can do."

Mackenzie ended the call and peered through the door. It was in the same disarray as the apartment building had been. She resisted the urge to break through the glass and unlock the door. Sure, there was no one around to see her do it, but it still wouldn't be right. She made her way around the block and found a back alley that ran behind each of the buildings along the block. When she came to the back of Parker Antiques, she found a sturdy door, locked and in decent condition. Having no other means to get inside, she pushed her morals aside and went back to the front. She used the butt of her gun as a club for the second time in half an hour, shattering the glass in the door just along the frame. She carefully snaked her arm into the break and slapped around the edge of the door for the deadbolt. She found it but had to give it a hard twist before it moved at all.

With the deadbolt disengaged, the door was still locked via the key slot. Rolling her eyes, Mackenzie again went a bit rogue. She took a step back and threw a hard kick into the frame just under the lock. The door frame cracked and the door went flying inward.

Mackenzie cringed and looked up and down the street to make sure no one had seen her.

With no witnesses, she walked into the store and closed the door behind her as best she could. At first glance, the breaking and entering had not been worth it. All of the cases were empty with the exception of more dust and cobwebs. While this space did smell much better than the apartment complex, there was still a thick scent of neglect in the air.

She walked behind the glass counters and old display cases and still saw nothing. There was an old flyer for a bake sale on the floor, stained with time and age. She also saw an old ring box, a nickel, and an assortment of dead insects on the ground. She explored the rest of the shop and found several cardboard boxes in the back. They were stuffed to the brim with old invoices, some dating back as far as 1982. All of the invoices showed a header with a very simple *Parker Antiques* logo.

She could go through all of the boxes but knew that the chances of finding anything worthwhile would be very small. She walked back up to the recently damaged front door and looked out. She could see the large window in the office of the apartment building. She imagined her father's silhouette there, behind that old desk, doing work.

The businesses are just too close to not be a coincidence. We're just one letter off...Parker and Barker. Something sure as hell doesn't add up here.

She checked her watch. It was 3:40; only twelve minutes had passed since she'd called Harrison with her request. He was fast, but not quite that fast. To occupy her time, Mackenzie ventured into the back rooms of the store. She assumed they had been to hold inventory that had just come in or goods that weren't selling. She found more scattered paraphernalia in the rooms: an old baseball card pricing guide, the back to an earring, several clothes hangers.

On a shelf in the second small room she checked, she found a small cardboard box. The top had been removed and the bottom sat securely within it. Inside, several small cards lay slanted against the back, coated in dust.

Business cards...

She drew a sharp breath as she saw that someone had placed an assortment of old business cards in the box—a poor man's Rolodex. There looked to be roughly thirty or so in all. She thumbed through them and passed by business cards for local businesses like auto shops, insurance companies, computer repair shops, and construction companies. Then, at the back of the box, she saw something that made her pause.

The last cards in the box were old unused business cards for Parker Antiques.

They looked identical to the ones she'd been obsessing over as of late, labeled *Barker Antiques*.

These had the same font, the same layout, the same cardstock. Identical, except the B was a P.

"What the hell?" she said.

Holding the cards, she did see *one* difference. These cards had one extra line. It was the final line on the card, written in small type.

531-555-6077 / Tim Parker, Owner

There was only one number, indicating that it was likely a landline given the look of the store. She doubted the place had still been open when cell phones had quickly taken over the world.

She pulled out her phone and dialed Harrison again.

"Nothing yet," Harrison said. "I have the IRS looking into it. I figured they could pull tax records and get you everything you need."

"Cancel it," Mackenzie said. "I think I found what I need right here. One more request for you, though. Can you find the current address and career information for a man named Tim Parker, originally from the Elm Branch region?"

"Oh yeah, that's much easier. Give me about five minutes."

After ending the call, Mackenzie pocketed one of the business cards. Just to be sure, she tried the number on the card. After a few clicks, she received a message telling her that the number was no longer in service.

She examined the rest of the store and found nothing of interest. If there was anything at all to take away, it was just how quickly a lot of smaller towns in America had gone under in such an alarmingly short period of time sometime in the early nineties. Blame it on the Internet or larger companies setting up shop in nearby cities…but it was an unavoidable fact.

True to his word, Harrison called her back six minutes later. "Tim Parker," he said. "Current residence is 664 Moore Road. Right there in Elm Branch."

"Awesome. Thanks, Harrison."

It occurred to her as she hurried out of the store that Harrison had become something of a go-to—a very reliable source of information that she was taking for granted.

Sort of the same way you're taking Ellington for granted, she thought.

But she did not have time for that thought to bog her down. As she hurried to her car, she could practically feel those business cards in her pocket, weighing her down as if they were not just little pieces of cardstock, but a bomb ticking away next to her skin, threatening to explode at any moment.

CHAPTER TWENTY ONE

Another great thing about small towns that Mackenzie had forgotten all about was the close proximity to everything. She was able to make the trip from the abandoned Parker Antiques building to the home of Tim Parker in less than ten minutes. She wondered if it was depressing in a way, to live out the rest of your life ten minutes away from the shell of a business you had been unable to keep afloat.

When she pulled into the dirt driveway of the small house that had been built to mimic a farmhouse style, she saw a man sitting in a rocker on the porch. There was a weed eater propped up in his lap as he worked at the head of it. As she turned in, the man looked up at her while still tinkering with his work.

Mackenzie made it halfway up his cracked sidewalk before his stare got to her and she had to speak.

"Are you Mr. Parker?" she asked. "Tim Parker?"

"I am," he said. "And if you're selling something, you might as well stop right there and go back to your car."

"No, I'm not selling anything," she said, pulling out her ID. "I'm Agent Mackenzie White, with the FBI. I was hoping you had the time for me to ask you a few questions."

"About what?" he asked.

"Well, may I come up on your porch?"

"Yeah," he said. "Maybe you can figure out what's wrong with this damned weed eater."

"Doubtful," she said, doing her best to seem as cheerful as possible. It was obvious from the start that Tim Parker was a typical grumpy old man—likely pushing about seventy-five or so and with no clear direction of what to do now that he was apparently retired.

He eyed her suspiciously, looking her up and down in a non-sexual way. "FBI? In this nothing little town?"

"Yes, sir. I understand that at one point in time, you owned Parker Antiques. Is that correct?"

"It is. Ran that little place for about twenty years or so. We did pretty well for a few years but then Amazon snuck up on everyone. Amazon…eBay…it was impossible to keep up."

"When did you finally go out of business?"

"Fall of 2002. I ended up selling what was left at rates that made me lose money in the end. But I was luckier than some, I know that for sure."

"Directly across from your store, there was an apartment complex. Do you remember that?"

"Yeah. It was a hellhole. I think it went through four or five different landlords before it just became too much to maintain. The building was always a heap. It just cost more money than it was worth to keep repairing it."

"Did you know all of the landlords?" Mackenzie asked.

"No, just the last two, I think. I actually went to high school with the final guy. He died of a heart attack three years ago...but the building had been condemned long before that. Now...please forgive me, but what does this all have to do with anything?"

Mackenzie reached into her pocket and took out the business card she had taken from the box in the back of the store less than half an hour ago. She handed it to Tim and he took it with a thin smile.

"This was your old business card, right?" she asked.

"It was."

She watched his face, looking for any indication that the sight of the card made him nervous. As hard as it was for her to imagine it, she *was* aware that his connection to this business card could very well make him a suspect. But she saw nothing other than a sad sort of remembrance in his expression as he looked at the business card.

Mackenzie then took out her phone, scrolled through a few photos, and brought up a picture of one of the Barker Antiques cards. She showed it to him and when he had to squint to see it, she simply handed the phone to him.

"How about this one? Does this look familiar to you?"

Again, she watched for any signs of panic or fear and saw none. In fact, his reaction confused her. He nodded his head and let out a little chuckle of amusement.

"What?" Mackenzie asked.

"Yeah, it looks familiar. When I decided I needed business cards, I called up this place in North Platte to get some printed. Had no idea what I was doing. I ordered them one day and they came in the mail about two weeks later—another thing the Internet sped up, of course. So I got 'em and that's how they turned out. They misspelled my damn name. My wife also pointed out that I was dumb not to include my name and the phone number. So I had to order new ones," he said, holding up the one she had taken from the store.

"And what did you do with the misprints?" Mackenzie asked.

"I ended up giving them away. My wife and I were talking about the terrible experience with that print place in North Platte, talking about the unusable cards. Some guy was in the store at that time and asked if he could have them. Said he'd use the blank sides for note-taking and stuff like that. I thought it was dumb, honestly, but I wasn't using them. So I gave them to him."

"Do you know when this was?"

Tim thought hard for a moment and then shrugged. "Maybe 1985? I'm not sure. But surely no later than '87."

"By any chance, do you happen to remember the man you gave the cards to?"

"Not personally, no."

"No name?" she asked. "Nothing about his appearance?"

"Sorry, no. All I can tell you was that it was a white guy, probably in his late twenties or early thirties. It *was* a guy I had seen from time to time, though."

"So he lived in Elm Branch?"

"Oh yeah."

"How can you be so sure?"

"Well…you mentioned that apartment complex across the street from the shop. The guy lived there, in one of those apartments."

Chills raced through Mackenzie and it was hard to breathe for a moment.

The man that left these cards at the murder scenes lived in the same apartment complex my father managed for a few years, she thought. *Hell…he might have been living there* when *my father was running it.*

"You okay, young lady?" Tim asked.

Mackenzie blinked the thought away. The circle was closing, maybe had already closed, and she was closer than ever now.

"Yes, I'm fine," she said rather absently. She gave him one of her own business cards, trying to be polite but also anxious to get moving again. "Thank you for your time," she added. "Please call me if you can think of anything else about the man you gave those cards to. It could prove very helpful in a case that's been unsolved for almost twenty years. And good luck with your weed eater."

Tim nodded and looked rather sad—perhaps because he was unable to remember anything much about the man he had given the cards to. He gave her a little wave as Mackenzie hurried back down his sidewalk and toward her car.

Back behind the wheel, she was visibly trembling. A million scenarios raced through her head, but one of them struck her as almost impossible, yet fitting.

The killer, with those misprinted cards, walking through the halls to his apartment...maybe passing my father somewhere along the way. Smiling. Waving. Maybe plotting something...

"But why?" she whispered to herself.

With that question cemented into her head, she peeled out of Tim Parker's driveway and headed back to Belton.

CHAPTER TWENTY TWO

With no field office or motel room to go to, Mackenzie settled for the motel parking lot, sure she'd end up getting a room there for the night anyway. She took her laptop out of its case, powered it up, and then called Ellington, requesting a FaceTime call. Tension and mixed emotions be damned, the case had to come first. And finally, it seemed to be moving along with rocket speed.

Ellington answered, his voice sounding hopeful and a bit tired. She could also see a bit of fatigue in his eyes but it was also unmistakable that he was happy to see her face. "Hey," he said. "To start this conversation off, I'd just like to let you know how fucked up it was that you waited for me to leave the room and then went off on your own crusade. Can we agree to that?"

"Yes," she said. "And I'm sorry. I just don't—"

"How are things in Belton?" he asked, cutting her off.

He's pissed, she thought. *My God, I ruined this, didn't I?*

"After a trip to a nearby little town called Elm Branch, things are looking pretty exciting, actually," she said. She did her best to match his mood, trying to pretend that there wasn't this huge tension between them.

"How so?" he asked.

She held up Tim Parker's old card to the screen and showed it to him. He took a moment to understand what he was seeing but in an instant, all of the fatigue seemed to leave his face.

"Holy shit," he said. "That's a real place?"

"Yeah. Closed down for many years now, but it's still there. I talked to Tim Parker and that's where things got interesting. I need you to gather up Penbrook and his team and patch me through for a conference call. How soon can you make that happen?"

"Penbrook is with Forensics right now but I can have him in a conference room within about fifteen minutes."

"Perfect. Call me back when things are set up and ready to go."

While she waited for the callback, Mackenzie weighed her options. She could play the role of the responsible agent and head back to Omaha to be with the rest of the team as they analyzed and pored over all of this new information. Or she could stay in Belton—which, honestly, seemed like the more fruitful choice. She

114

felt obligated to stay in the location that had offered up the most promising leads on the case. If Penbrook wanted to get snotty about it, she could deal with that. And given everything that had happened to this point, she was pretty sure Ellington would understand and support her decision even after the stunt she had pulled on him.

Given that, she went to the front office and booked a room for the night. She set up her laptop and waited for the call from Ellington. As she waited, an itching thought kept recurring, coming to her like a fly buzzing around her head. It involved Dennis Parks and his connection with her father. Parks had been a policeman for a year and then quit the force. According to reports, he just wasn't cut out for the job. He ended up selling homes in Morrill County, dabbling here and there in real estate.

Her phone rang, ending that stream of thought. When the call came, she directed it to her laptop and took a seat on the edge of the bed.

When she answered, she saw Ellington, Penbrook, and two other agents she had seen around the field office all huddled around the conference room table. Ellington looked more excited than the others, perhaps because he'd caught a few details from Mackenzie before setting up the call.

"You've made some progress, I hear?" Penbrook asked.

"I have." She then went on to tell them about the things she had discovered throughout the day—discovering the business cards in Parker Antiques and then her conversation with Tim Parker. As she made her way through the recollection, she could see a dawning excitement on Penbrook's face. She knew the feeling well; finally, this damned case seemed to be going somewhere.

"Okay," Penbrook said. "So let's take a bird's-eye view of what we have. Agent White, this is essentially your baby. Where do you want to start?"

"Well, based on what Tim Parker told me, we know that the man that took those misprinted business cards was living in the apartment complex sometime between 1984 and 1987. We need to somehow get a list of all tenants in that building during that timeframe. I'd also like to find out who the landlord was during that time. Sadly enough, I feel pretty confident that it was my father. And if that's the case, that's obviously going to lead nowhere. I just need to confirm it for sure."

"Sounds like an excellent plan of attack," Penbrook said. "You do realize that compiling such a list is going to take some time."

"I do," she said. "And once you have that list, I'd like for your team to simplify it. People that are deceased need to be removed from it. We need it as small as possible when I get it. Any addresses or criminal records that are available, I need those as well."

"Anything else?" Ellington asked.

"I think that's it for now. While you guys work that angle, I think I might reach back out to the Scotts family to see if there's something we missed. In light of these new discoveries, it might be worth a shot. Maybe dig around the Hambry case, too."

"Sounds good," Penbrook said. "We'll let you know as soon as we find some names for tenants. Let us know if you need anything else on our end."

With that send-off, Mackenzie checked her watch. It was quickly approaching six o'clock, which made things a little more difficult in terms of reaching out to the Scotts family. She hated to feel as if she was throwing Kim Scotts's grieving in her face, but at this point she didn't have much of a choice. She assumed, though, that she could do the woman a favor and call rather than just drop by and expect her to be polite and cordial.

She pulled the reports up on her laptop, located Kim Scotts's contact information, and placed the call. She was fully prepared for anger from Kim's end and, honestly, felt she deserved it.

Kim Scotts answered on the third ring with a bit of cheer in her voice. "Hello?"

"Hi, Mrs. Scotts? This is Mackenzie White with the FBI. I spoke with you the—"

"I remember," Kim said, the cheer instantly dropped from her voice. "And while I know you are only doing your job, I thought I made it clear that I'm really trying to leave all of this in the past."

"You did. And I'm sorry. But we made some progress today that might lead to discovery of the suspect's name. I promise you...I have only one question for you right now and that's it."

Kim sighed and said, "Fine. But make it quick. I'm right in the middle of making dinner."

"While your husband was alive, did either of you have any connection at all to the town of Elm Branch?"

There was a brief silence on Kim's end of the line. "Yeah, I think Jimmy might have lived there for a bit sometime before we met. I'm pretty sure of it, actually."

"Do you know where?"

"No. I don't know exactly where."

Mackenzie thought she could maybe push it a bit more but she didn't want to run the risk of completely souring things with Kim Scotts, who could still probably provide some valuable information depending on where the case led.

116

Besides, the fact that Kim was fairly certain that Jimmy had once lived in Elm Branch was really all that Mackenzie was looking for. And while it did not blow a single lead wide open, it *did* widen out a thread...a thread that seemed promising, but that Mackenzie was not ready to put all of her chips on just yet. She thanked Kim and ended the call.

She still had some digging to do. And while the constant research and studying of notes seemed almost like a waste of time, she was disciplined enough to know that sometimes cases were cracked in the form of relentlessly studying case files; it didn't always come down to chasing a suspect down with a gun.

Maybe that's why I'm so frustrated, she thought. *I feel inactive...like the files and reports are weighing me down.*

She looked at her laptop and all of the material gathered on the bed and the small table her laptop sat on. There *had* to be answers in there. She just had to find them.

With a heavy sigh and a dulled sense of motivation, Mackenzie returned to the material and started digging again.

CHAPTER TWENTY THREE

Mackenzie was mostly nude when someone knocked on the door at 11:45. She was in the midst of stripping down to her sleeping attire when the rapping at the door startled her. She looked at the door, curious and a little concerned. Other than Ellington, Penbrook, and the man who had checked her into the room earlier, no one knew she was there,

The knock came again. "Agent Mackenzie White?" came a man's voice. "If you're in there, please open the door. My name is Sheriff David Fredericks. I spoke with an Agent Ellington that told me you were staying here."

Mackenzie pulled her pants back on and ventured over to the door. She looked through the peephole and did indeed see a man in a sheriff's outfit. A female officer was with him, standing behind him. As she took them both in through the peephole, her phone rang from behind her.

"One moment," she called.

She checked the phone display and saw that it was Ellington...probably calling to tell her to be prepared for a visit from the Belton sheriff. She silenced the ringer and went back to the door. She opened it slowly and waved Sheriff Fredericks inside.

"What can I do for you, Sheriff?" she asked.

Fredericks and the woman—Officer Potter, by the name on her breastplate—stepped into the room, Potter closing the door behind her.

"We've got a body that we are pretty certain is linked to a case that you are currently working. Agent Ellington gave us the details when we spoke to him."

"Why did you call the bureau in the first place?" Mackenzie asked.

"Because of the business card we found on the body. Barker Antiques. The PD has known about the open case for a while now. Everyone on the force has been instructed to call the FBI right away if they so much as *think* they're reporting on a crime that is connected to it. I called the field office in Omaha and they directed me to Agent Ellington...who told me you were here."

"Any ID on the body?" she asked. "Was it a vagrant or homeless person?"

"No," he said sourly. "Quite the opposite, actually. The crime scene is only about fifteen minutes away from here. I was hoping you'd come out with us and have a look."

"Any indication how long the body has been there?" she asked.

Again, Fredericks made that grim expression. "Not long at all. When we got there, the blood was still flowing."

The killer is here, Mackenzie thought. *No longer in Omaha...in Belton. But why? And how long has he been here?*

"Let's go," she said.

She grabbed up her sidearm and ID off of the dresser and marched out of the room behind Fredericks and Potter. As she took the passenger seat of Fredericks's cruiser, she could hear police sirens in the distance. While the sound likely made most people cringe with worry, she couldn't help but feel relieved by it. Sure, there had been another murder and that was certainly tragic.

But blaring police sirens on the move meant things were happening—that a case was, in way or another, evolving and hopefully coming closer to its end.

***

The crime scene was along the side of State Route 14, which drove through both Belton and Elm Branch. When Fredericks pulled the car over where a few other patrol cars were parked with their flashers on, they were a bit closer to Elm Branch than Belton. A strange feeling passed through Mackenzie when she realized she had passed this very spot no more than twelve hours ago...a little less, actually.

She got out of the car and walked further out along the road, flanked by Fredericks and Potter. The body was lying about eight feet off of the road, casually dumped in a gathering of weeds and scrubby trees. Mackenzie could tell at once that it was a female even though it was lying face down in the weeds.

"The victim is Wanda Young," Fredericks said. "She's a longtime Belton resident who left for a few years to do some mission work in Africa after her husband died. She's been back home for about six months. Everyone made a big deal about it because her family comes from money. It was like the golden child returning home."

"Has anyone moved the body?" Mackenzie asked.

"The first officer on the scene pulled her shoulder up just enough to see her face, just to get the ID. That's also when he saw the business card. Other than that, she'd gone untouched."

Mackenzie approached the body and hunkered down next to it. Wanda Young had been wearing a thin Under Armour windbreaker when she had died. Mackenzie very carefully lifted the body partially by the shoulder. She was pretty in a plain way and looked to be forty or fifty. There was a clear fracture to the side of her head on the left side. A heavy gash sat below it, still trickling out blood.

Fresh, Mackenzie thought. *This murder took place no more than an hour ago. Maybe even less.*

Wanda's eyes were still open and her mouth was slightly agape. The Barker Antiques business card had been stuffed into her mouth. It was hard to tell from the angle and the poor light, but she thought it had been folded perfectly in half.

"Can someone get me some better light and something to get the card out with?" she called back over her shoulder.

At once, two officers were standing behind her with flashlights—Potter on her right and another officer on her left. A few seconds later, Fredericks handed her a pair of tweezers. He also handed her a thin set of plastic evidence gloves. Mackenzie put the gloves on and carefully pried the card away from Wanda Young's mouth.

Behind her, she heard a man utter the words *holy shit.* This was followed by a slight commotion. Before examining the card, Mackenzie turned to see what was going on. One of the other officers was quickly approaching Fredericks, holding a cell phone.

"Sheriff…we've got a witness."

"To the murder?"

"Yeah, we think so," the officer said, "Or her abduction prior to the murder at least."

Fredericks looked at Mackenzie, giving her a shrug and a look that conveyed the question: *You want to take it?*

Mackenzie got to her feet, removed the evidence gloves, and took the cell phone. "This is Agent Mackenzie White with the FBI," she recited. "Who's speaking?"

"My name is Amanda Napier," an obviously upset woman said.

"And you're calling the police why exactly?"

"About an hour ago…I saw someone attack a friend of mine— a woman named Wanda Young."

"And where are you calling from?" Mackenzie asked.

"My home in Belton."

"And where did you see the attack?"

Amanda paused here, sniffling a sob away. "Outside of Wanda's house. She lives in that really nice two-story on Felton Street. When I saw her, she was heading up her porch stairs and someone…someone grabbed her. Hit her hard. He had something in his hand."

"And what did you do?"

"Nothing…I…I shouldn't have been there. I—"

As Amanda Napier broke down, Sheriff Fredericks approached Mackenzie. He looked like he might be sick. He was clearly worried and unsettled—even more so than he had been when he had given her the identity of Wanda Young.

"What is it?" she mouthed.

Fredericks showed her that he was holding the business card that she had tweezed out of Wanda's mouth. He had unfolded it and was currently showing her the back of it.

Something was written there, in all capital letters in black ink. The handwriting was sloppy and intentionally childish in nature.

But there was nothing at all childish about the message.

WELCOME HOME, AGENT WHITE.

CHAPTER TWENTY FOUR

Mackenzie thanked Sheriff Fredericks for his assistance and asked to have a policeman escort her back to the motel, where she instantly got into her own car and called Ellington. He answered right away, sounding very angry.

"What gives with you not answering your fucking phone?" he growled at her. "I was worried absolutely sick!"

"The killer is here in Belton," she said. "He left a little note for me on the back of the latest business card. Things are moving wide open here right now and I didn't have time to call you with updates until now. Is that okay?"

"A note? What kind of note?"

She briefly told him about the crime scene and what they had found on the back of the business card after Fredericks had unfolded it. As she recounted it, it still sent a chill through her and she had to once again remind herself of the very dire facts that had all come to surface in the last half an hour or so.

The killer is here in Belton. And he knows I'm here. But why taunt me? Is he trying to get my attention? Will he come for me next?

"So you have a good feeling that the case, for whatever reason, is basically relocated now? The killer is there, the most recent death is there...Belton is the hotspot?"

"Seems that way."

"I'm coming out there then."

She nearly argued against it, wanting to stress the importance of having his presence at the field office. But it made sense—both logically and for her own well-being.

"Maybe get some sleep first," she said, realizing already that this was going to be a sleepless night for her.

"You're a fine one to talk. Any leads yet?"

"We got a witness that placed a call about twenty minutes ago. I'm heading over to speak with her right now. She seemed legitimately upset. I think it might just lead to something."

"Sounds promising. Look...just don't go all commando on this, okay? Please be careful."

"I will," she said, warmed by the concern.

She ended the call and pulled up the address Amanda Napier had left when she was on the phone. Fredericks had agreed to meet Mackenzie at the residence as soon as possible but Mackenzie didn't see the point in waiting. She pulled out of the motel lot and started the short seven-minute journey to Amanda's house.

It was 12:26 in the morning and for Mackenzie, the day was already well underway.

***

To her surprise, Sheriff Fredericks was already walking up onto Amanda Napier's stoop when she pulled into the driveway. It was a smaller house but looked rather nice—among the nicer ones she had seen in her return to Belton. He waited for her as she stepped out of the car but he seemed in no particular hurry. He was pushing sixty and had the sort of face that showed very little emotion. It was difficult to tell exactly how he felt in the moment but she had to assume it would be the typical small-town cop reaction to a grisly murder.

"We'll have to confirm to be sure," Fredericks said, "but it looks like Wanda Young was hit with some sort of hammer or dull ax. Twice in the side of the head and then again in the stomach. The one to the stomach went deep. Looks like it got the intestines."

Mackenzie logged the information into her brain, nodded, and then knocked on Amanda Napier's front door. Mackenzie could hear her approaching footsteps right away.

"One more thing," Fredericks said. "I know Amanda fairly well. If you'd let me start the questions, it might go easier. You're more than welcome to finish it out."

Mackenzie did not have time to respond. Amanda answered the door right away. It was clear that she had been crying. But she also looked at odds about something. She looked from Fredericks to Mackenzie, back and forth like she was waiting for one of them to punish her for something. She then seemed to shake off whatever strange fugue had carried her to the door and invited them in with a wave of her arm.

Amanda led them into her living room, a plush and nicely decorated space filled with books and pillows. Amanda plopped down on her couch and hugged a pillow closely to her. Mackenzie assumed the woman was in her early thirties, though it was hard to tell with the redness around her eyes and the overall disheveled state she was in.

123

"Amanda," Fredericks said, "I want to give you one more opportunity to tell me how you ended up seeing what happened to Wanda. Can you do that?"

Amanda nodded but it was clear that she didn't want to. Mackenzie studied her mannerisms as she responded to Fredericks and it was clear that she was hiding something. Every red flag available went up in Mackenzie's mind.

"I saw her going up her stairs, going into her house. And then someone came out of nowhere and just sort of...attacked her. I saw one punch...maybe two."

"Was there anything in the man's hand?" Mackenzie asked.

"I think so, but I couldn't see what it was."

"Quite frankly, Amanda," Fredericks said, "I'm not sure how you saw *anything*. Wanda's house is off the road quite a ways. I know you see the side of it from the road, but not the porch. Not unless I'm sorely mistaken. But I think for you to have seen such an event take place, you would have to have been in her driveway."

Mackenzie watched as Amanda's eyes dropped to the floor. Her shoulders also went tense and her fingers visibly squeezed at the pillow she was holding.

"What's going on, Amanda?" Fredericks said. "What happened to Wanda is a tragedy for sure but there's more to it. We believe she's the latest victim of a man that has killed several people. So if you know anything else, you need to tell us now."

Amanda looked back up at them, as if verifying what Fredericks had said was true. When she saw honesty in both their faces, her bottom lip quivered.

"Sheriff Fredericks...you can't tell anyone. It could ruin me if..."

"What is it?" Fredericks asked. He kept a calm, cool, and collected voice. It reminded Mackenzie of a doctor with an excellent bedside manner, trying his best to convey bad news in a way that was not heartbreaking.

"I *was* in her driveway. I had just dropped her off."

"You two were together tonight?"

"Yes. We...we were sort of seeing each other in private."

"Seeing?" Fredericks said, as if he had never heard the word before. He seemed genuinely baffled, so Mackenzie thought she should help before it got any more awkward.

"Amanda, do you mean that you and Wanda were seeing one another intimately?"

Amanda nodded. When Fredericks saw this acknowledgment, it was his turn to look at the floor. Mackenzie was pretty sure his face had also flushed a bit. He sighed, looked over to Mackenzie, and gave her a nod of approval to go ahead.

"How long had this been going on?" she asked.

"Maybe two months. We'd usually meet here because I'm sort of a nobody. Thirty-two years old and divorced. But Wanda came from money and has this stellar reputation. Mission work through the church. No one ever says a bad word about her. So I'd usually pick her up at her house or at some random location in town. Sometimes we'd spring for a room at the hotel."

"And tonight…she was here?" Mackenzie asked.

"Yes."

"When did you leave here to drop her off?"

"I don't remember. But I do remember the time when I saw what happened at her house. I checked the clock on my dashboard because I knew I was going to have to call the police. It was eleven thirteen."

"And when you saw what was happening on her porch steps, what did you do?" Mackenzie asked.

"I got out of the car and took a few steps. I called out, something stupid. Something like *hey, stop!* I don't remember, really. But then I heard the sound…like someone punching something really hard…it made me think of someone throwing a steak down on a plate." She gasped here, took a breath, and then went on with a tremor in her voice. "I heard that and knew it was too late. So I ran back to my car and hauled ass out of there."

"And why did you wait so long to call the police?" Mackenzie asked.

"Because I felt like a coward. And because…I wasn't sure how to do it. I was too worried about what people would think if they found out. I know that's selfish, but it's the truth and I'm sorry."

"Did you see the assailant clearly?"

"I never saw his face," Amanda said. "He was wearing one of those costume-type mask things. But I'm pretty sure I saw some hair coming out the back of it, like he had a mullet. Looked like he had an average build. And his clothes were pretty ratty. It made me think he was the type of guy that probably hadn't bathed in days, you know?"

The living room went quiet for a moment as Mackenzie and Fredericks let this sink in.

"Amanda," Fredericks said with that same slow assurance back in his voice. "Please understand…we're talking about Wanda Young. I can make sure the news doesn't go public, but for this story to hold up…is there any proof of the relationship?"

125

Amanda's face seemed to tighten as she nodded and looked at the floor again. "We filmed ourselves. Twice. One of those times was at the motel. We used her iPad to do it, so I'm not sure where it's saved. Maybe on her iCloud or her computer."

"You're sure of this?" Fredericks asked.

"Pretty sure, yeah."

"Forgive me for asking," Mackenzie said. "You said you're thirty-two. And Wanda was what…at least fifty?"

"Fifty exactly," Amanda said.

"Given her stature in the town and the age difference, I have to ask: was it a mutual relationship?"

"Yeah. It was. We were just…having fun at first. But then it was something more and it started to feel dangerous—but real, you know?"

"And do you happen to know what her mission trips were about?" Mackenzie asked.

"Construction projects somewhere near Zimbabwe, I believe. She was already talking about going back out there sometime next year."

Mackenzie nodded and looked back toward the front door. She was pretty sure that at some point, someone would have to look for the videos of Amanda and Wanda. But that was not pertinent for tonight as far as Mackenzie was concerned. She could tell from her emotional state and the embarrassing details she had shared that Amanda Napier had no involvement at all in the murder.

"Thank you, Amanda," Mackenzie said. "Sheriff, would you mind speaking with me outside?"

Fredericks got up and followed Mackenzie outside where they stood on the small front porch. They whispered among themselves in the quiet of the night as 1:00 a.m. came and went.

"She's innocent of just about everything," Mackenzie said. "I'd place a bet on it."

"Same here," Fredericks said. "And she wasn't kidding; if news of their affair got out in this town, she'd be shunned. And Wanda's name would be run through the mud."

"You were right about needing the proof," Mackenzie said. "Why don't you just hand this to the FBI as part of the case I'm on, since it's obviously part of it. We'll handle searching for the videos to clear her from it all. Washes your hands of it and keeps the town in the dark. No risk of someone on your force spreading gossip."

"Probably for the best," Fredericks said.

"For now, I'm going to head back to the motel. I need to update my partner and look through some files. Ca you handle things here?"

"Sure. And thanks for your help."

Mackenzie shook his hand and then went to the car. While she did plan on filling in Ellington and then looking back through the files for anything related to mission work, homosexuality, or the names Amanda Napier and Wanda Young, there was a much more prominent reason for going back.

She was haunted by the sight of the message on the business card that had come from Wanda's mouth.

WELCOME HOME, AGENT WHITE.

Someone was welcoming her back home. And a welcome typically meant there would be a meeting at some point.

She wasn't sure where it would happen or when, but Mackenzie would be damned sure she was ready for it.

CHAPTER TWENTY FIVE

By 2:40 that morning, Mackenzie had taken part in moving the body of Wanda Young and corroborating with officers on the scene. She requested that the official autopsy report be emailed to her, but it was clear that Fredericks's assessment of the cause of death had been correct: a deep cut to the stomach which had pierced the intestines and two heavy blows to the head, one of which had exposed a portion of skull.

When she arrived back at the motel, she knew she should be tired but she was actually quite invigorated. She did, however, make her way into the motel's office and politely requested that the clerk brew a pot of coffee for her since there were no individual mini pots in the rooms.

While she waited for the coffee to brew, she went into her room and phoned Ellington. She was glad to see that he sounded tired when he answered the phone, a clear indication that he had taken her advice and remained in Omaha for a few extra hours of sleep. She filled him in on what had occurred so far and they made plans to meet up sometime tomorrow in Belton around noon.

Then, in keeping with what she had told Sherriff Fredericks, she pored over all of the files she had so far. She reread the reports on her father, Gabriel Hambry, Jimmy Scotts, and Dennis Parks while drinking the bitter coffee that the helpful clerk brought to her room. She saw nothing in them that tied into the story they knew so far about Wanda Young. Seeing no clear connection, Mackenzie started to compile a list. She wrote down the names of each non-vagrant victim and tried to work it out like a puzzle.

My father, Benjamin White: failed landlord turned police officer; might have worked undercover on some sort of drug ring bust that there are no records of.

Jimmy Scotts: worked with a small marketing firm. Might have worked a job or two concerning community involvement. Killed in the exact same way as my father.

Gabriel Hambry: no known family living in the area. Lived in crummy part of Omaha and seemed to have no apparent job at the time of his death.

Dennis Parks: knew my father from a brief (failed?) stint as a police officer in training. When that didn't cut it, he tried his hand at real estate. Killed in the same way as my father, right down to staging the deceased wife on the couch in the living room.

Wanda Young: first female victim. Mission work in Africa involving construction. Comes from a wealthy family. Involved in secret affair with younger local woman.

She looked each listing over for connections. There were a few, but nothing that really stuck out and demanded attention. For instance, her father had tried his hand at being a landlord and Dennis Parks later worked in real estate. Not the same jobs overall, but similar in their roots. Another flimsy connection was Jimmy Scotts working a marketing job to promote community betterment while Wanda Young had been involved in mission work. Again…the same overall principle but not exactly a match.

There's got to be something that connects them all, Mackenzie thought as she pored over the list.

Her concentration was broken when her phone rang. She first looked at the clock, surprised to see that it was already 4:10 in the morning. She was then further surprised when she saw that the call was from McGrath.

Before she could speak a single word, McGrath was on the attack. It didn't scare her as much as it once had now that she knew him better and was aware that deep down, he did have her best interests and eventual success at heart. Still, hearing McGrath in a bad mood was not pleasant at all.

"You've been traveling a lot, haven't you?" he accused.

"I have, sir. But I think—"

"You and Ellington were assigned to assist in Omaha. Belton was nowhere on the radar."

"I'm aware of that, sir. But the investigation led me out here. And consequently, it seems that the killer is now here as well."

"I'm aware. I got the call from Ellington. Maybe that was a call you should have made…had you been in Omaha."

"With all due respect, sir, with the killer here, I'd be useless in Omaha."

"I agree. Makes you wonder…maybe the killer is there because you are there."

"I'm beginning to believe that as well, sir."

"Why is that?"

She then updated him on everything she knew—about the personal message to her on the back of the business card that had been pulled from Wanda Young's mouth, in particular.

When she was done, McGrath let out a sigh. "I want you to level with me, White. I want one hundred percent honesty on this next question. Understand?" He paused and then dropped it on her. "Are you too close to this?"

"Probably closer than I should be," she admitted. "But I'm getting close now, sir. And even if I wasn't...I feel like he's coming for me now. Like he knows we're on to him and he's almost taunting me...trying to tease me or lure me out."

"If you were anyone else, I'd pull you from this. I'll tell you right now: I've told Ellington to keep tabs on you. If he feels that you're too emotionally connected to do a good job, he's going to call me. And if that happens, I *will* pull you from the case. And not just for a while...for good."

"I understand," Mackenzie said. And she *did*. She was simply thankful that he was allowing her to stay on.

"Good. Now do what you can to make sure this stays and *ends* in Belton. Got it?"

He hung up before she could respond...which was par for the course when it came to phone conversations with McGrath.

Mackenzie used the break in analyzing the records and reports to call Fredericks to see if there were any developments on his end. He had nothing new for her, only his assurance that he had nearly his entire department staking out the town for anything that raised even the tiniest bit of suspicion. He also ended the conversation with a vow to call her right away if anything came up.

Realizing that she had only grabbed about two hours of rest in the last thirty-six hours, she set an alarm on her phone for eighty minutes and lay down on the bed. She remained in her clothes, only kicking off her shoes.

She did not need the melatonin this time. Despite the anxiousness in her guts and the multitude of thoughts in her head, she managed to sink into a shallow sleep right away.

***

It was not her alarm that woke her up, but the ringing of her phone. Hoping that it was Sheriff Fredericks with an update, she answered it right away without looking at the display. She was instantly awake, the pull of the nap dissolving at once. But she also felt a dull and lurking pain in the back of her head, a feeling she knew all too well—a looming exhaustion headache.

"This is Agent White," she answered.

The voice on the other end did not belong to Fredericks, though. She was confused by it at first but then her mind locked it in.

"Hi, Agent White. This is Tim Parker. I know it's early, but I had a thought a few minutes ago and thought you might want to know it."

She glanced to the clock and saw that it was 5:55. An early time for most, sure, but not an older man who probably had a tendency to rise early. And certainly not early for an eager FBI agent who felt that she was nearing the tail end of a case.

"It's never too early," she said. "I appreciate the call. What do you have for me?"

"I woke up at a little after four this morning because I kept thinking about that man I gave the business cards to. I remember telling you that it wasn't the first time I'd seen him and that was true—but it snagged in my head. I was trying to figure out how I knew him...and then it hit me: he *did* buy something from me that day. I think he did it just to be nice because I'd given him the cards."

"And do you have any record of that transaction?" she asked.

"I do. I'm down at my old shop, looking at it right now. He bought a few books. Three hardcovers and an old *Field and Stream* magazine. He paid with a credit card, so I have the old receipt right here. His name is Greg Redman. Sadly, that's all I can give you."

Mackenzie was too excited to have a name to be bothered by Parker's last comment.

"What about the books?" she asked, wondering if the subject matter might provide some insights.

"No. I can't tell that from the receipt. They *are* all listed as general fiction, though."

"Anything else you can remember?" she asked.

"No, I'm afraid that's it."

"Don't sound so down about it," she said. "This is a massive help. Thank you so much for the call."

She ended the call and then picked up the phone to call Fredericks right away. He sounded exhausted when he answered the phone but his voice seemed to perk up when he realized that it was Mackenzie on the other end.

"I've got a name," Mackenzie told him, sharing the details of the call she'd just had with Tim Parker.

"It doesn't ring a bell," Fredericks said. "Do you know if he's a resident of Belton or Elm Branch?"

"No idea," she said.

"That's okay. We'll run the name here and see what we come up with."

"And I'll do the same on the bureau end," she added.

With a name, a fragile certainty that the killer was somewhere close by, and a sunrise pulling in another new day, Mackenzie's one-hour nap seemed to have been enough. After splashing some water in her face and making her hair at least somewhat presentable, she grabbed her ID and Glock. She tried to focus on these simple tasks, doing everything she could to ignore the creeping pain of the headache that was even now growing bit by bit.

As she headed for the door, someone knocked on it from the other side.

She peered through the peephole and couldn't help but smile. She opened it quickly and fought the urge to weep.

Ellington was standing there and the way a surge of relief flooded through her at the sight of him did two things: it made her feel that things between them were going to be just fine and it also made her feel much more confident in finding an end to this case.

She took his hand and pulled him inside. Without bothering to close the door behind him, Ellington allowed her to draw him in through the door. She pulled him to her with a bit of drama and clung to him.

"I'm so sorry," she said. "I don't know what the hell I'm doing."

She sobbed against him and while it was embarrassing, the vulnerability and absolute sense of letting go was a relief.

"You're wrestling your demons and, apparently, near the end of wrapping a case from the looks of it."

They smiled at one another, the smiles not faltering until their mouths met in a kiss that she didn't realize she had needed for the last two days or so.

When the kiss broke, she looked him directly in the eyes— something she found hard to do because of her aversion to vulnerability.

"I'm glad you're here," she said. "And I'm sorry if you felt like I pushed you away. This case...you called it *wrestling demons* a while ago. And that's exactly what it feels like. Again, I'm so sorry."

"Well, I don't accept your apology," he said. "Not right now, anyway. I don't even want you thinking about that nonsense until we get this case taken care of. Deal?"

She responded with another kiss. She broke it this time, refocusing her priorities...which was harder than normal to do now that he was standing directly in front of her.

"We got a name," she said.

"For the killer?"

She nodded. "And I feel like he's probably still here in town. Or maybe in the neighboring town of Elm Branch."

"Then let's go get the fucker," Ellington said.

They left the room and stepped out into the morning. Even before they made it to her car, Mackenzie saw two patrol cars flying down the road. Their sirens were not on, but they were easily breaking the speed limit, riding nearly bumper to bumper.

"You going to be okay with this?" Ellington asked, getting into the car. She could tell by the way he talked and the look of confidence on his face that he felt it, too—that one way or the other, this case was going to close soon, right here in Belton.

"With what?" she asked.

"Closing this case in Belton. With me. I mean, it almost seems like some sort of cosmic justice but still...I get how this can be a head trip for you."

"I'm fine," she said, well aware that she was lying a bit.

She was pretty sure Ellington picked up on it, too. But he said nothing as she started the car and pulled out into the highway, following behind the two patrol cars that had just blazed by.

CHAPTER TWENTY SIX

By eight o'clock that morning, Mackenzie found herself at the nexus of the case. She was serving as the liaison for the small police forces of Morrill County, three ragtag forces out of Belton and other small communities within the county. She was organizing and sending out teams to canvass the areas, looking for anyone with any background information on a man named Greg Redman. She was also working closely with the FBI—communicating with Penbrook in the Omaha field office and Harrison and Yardley out of the headquarters in DC.

She could also feel the headache she'd been sensing growing by leaps and bounds. She'd taken three ibuprofen shortly after leaving the motel but so far, it had done nothing.

It all had the feeling of finality, of some sort of massive storm that was gathering its clouds and building toward something catastrophic.

The first hope of some sort of break came in the form of a call from Harrison just after lunch. Mackenzie and Ellington were parked in the lot of the Belton Legion Hall when the call came in. The car smelled of hot coffee and fried breakfast foods from the diner in town—which had actually served to make Mackenzie more alert and energized.

"So here's what we've got on Greg Redman, former resident of Belton, Nebraska," Harrison said through the phone. "He moved from Belton to Seattle, Washington, in 1999. He worked as a call center stooge for one of those fraudulent places that reportedly help people get out of student loan debt. He lost his job there in 2002 when he got into some sort of altercation with a supervisor. After that, there's not much. We can see where he bought a plane ticket to Nicaragua in 2003 and then applied for a loan for a car in El Paso, Texas, in 2011…a loan he was denied for. That's where it dead-ends."

"So no history of Omaha?" Ellington asked.

"Nothing."

"What about existing family in the Belton or Elm Branch region?" Mackenzie asked.

"Nothing. His mother died when he was four and his father remarried. From what I see here, he's currently living in Connecticut."

"What about Nicaragua? Do we know why he went there?"

"No clue. And honestly, we have no idea how long he was there. I don't have records of when he came back into the country. Those records clearly have to exist somewhere, but we're still digging."

Mackenzie's phone got an incoming call, showing Fredericks's number on the display.

"Thanks, Harrison," she said. "But I have an incoming that I need to take. Keep up the good work and please keep us posted."

She switched over to the incoming call from Fredericks.

"Got something new?" Mackenzie asked.

"One of my officers ran into a man that knew your father," Fredericks said. "When they were talking, it was discovered that this guy new Gabriel Hambry."

"But Hambry was in Omaha," Mackenzie said. "The files show that he's lived there for at least ten years."

"That's exactly right," Fredericks said. "But I had another guy run a report and he discovered that Hambry moved to Belton with his family in 1977. When he got older, he moved out of Belton and rented a place in Elm Branch. Want to take a guess at where he lived?"

Click.

Mackenzie could almost literally feel something clicking into place within her head. *That's it,* she thought. *That's the connection. And maybe even the motive.*

"My father's apartment building."

"Bingo. Also…one other thing. We also did some digging into Wanda Young. I told you about how her family was basically made of money and she was typically thought of as this holier-than-thou moneybags type, right?"

"Yeah?"

"Well, she went through a rebellious streak in her early twenties. Wanted to piss Mommy and Daddy off. Dyed her hair. Slept around. But she didn't move far away. For a period of exactly a year and a half, she was also a resident of your father's apartment building."

From beside her, Ellington breathed, "Holy shit…"

"Do you think your guys can run—"

"I already have a small team assembled to see if we can put the rest of the pieces together," Fredericks said. "At the risk of seeming

135

bossy, I *will* say that they could maybe use some help if we want this knocked out quickly."

"We may just lend a hand," Mackenzie said. "Thanks, Sheriff."

She and Ellington looked at one another after the call, both absorbing what this latest revelation might mean. Ellington looked a bit alarmed.

"What's wrong?" he said.

"Nothing."

"I call bullshit. You look pale and you've been wincing a lot. Rubbing at your temples, too."

"It's just a headache. It'll pass."

"You need to rest. How much sleep have you had?"

She brushed the conversation away with a lazy sweep on her hand. "I'm going to go ahead and shatter the word *coincidence*," Mackenzie said, getting them back on track. "The killer lived there. Wanda Young and Gabriel Hambry lived there. Jimmy Scotts lived *somewhere* in Elm Branch...and as of right now, I'm betting on it being in those apartments."

"Do we have a definitive timeline of when your father owned and operated the building?" Ellington asked.

"No...but that's a damned good place to start."

***

By noon, she had placed a few more information requests. She had called Harrison and asked him to get the residence histories of Jimmy Scotts and Dennis Parks. She'd then called the field office in Omaha and spoken with Penbrook. He had his men digging into the state documents regarding land and property ownership and leasing to see how long Benjamin White had been in possession of the rental properties on Spruce Street in Elm Branch.

She and Ellington then joined three officers at the Belton PD, trying to expedite some of those requests by good old-fashioned hand-to-paper research. Mackenzie took the time to dig through the records and pull out her father's records, which were scattered here and there throughout the paper files and digital archives, though they were far from complete. She looked through his arrest records and reports, looking for any kind of an event that might have somehow involved him with someone with the capacity to be a serial killer.

The only questionable thing she came across was a very sketchy detail near the end of his career as a policeman. She supposed this was around the time he had possibly gone undercover. A few arrests before the lapse in his records, he had taken down three men who had been working toward getting roughly twenty pounds of heroin into Morrill County. In fact, if she took anything away from going through his career records, it was that he played a simple role in the law enforcement of the area, but he had done it well.

She also had one of the women who worked up front search the database for any criminal records pertaining to Gabriel Hambry, Dennis Parks, or Jimmy Scotts. The only pings she got back were an overdue parking ticket from Parks and a drunk and disorderly from Jimmy Scotts. The drunk and disorderly came from just five years ago, long after his time in Elm Branch was over.

However, a knock on the door to the small records room ended up giving her much more information and insight. It was an officer who had been very diligent in helping Mackenzie and Ellington find the records they needed. He was a younger guy who seemed over the moon to help in their investigation.

"We've got an ID on one of the vagrants from Omaha," he said.

"Did you get a call from Washington on that?" Mackenzie asked.

"No," he said, shaking his head. "We found it here in the office but then reached out to your friend Agent Harrison for photo confirmation."

"So you're saying one of the vagrants from Omaha was a local?"

"Yeah. A guy named Sam Hudson. He lost his job here back in 2013. We're not sure how he ended up in Omaha but we're ninety percent sure he was one of the more recent ones to be killed. And if it *does* turn out to be him, we think the younger vagrant—the twelve-year-old—was his son. Your people in DC are confirming right now."

"Can you get me a physical address for his time here in Belton?" she asked.

"We're pulling it right now," he said.

Mackenzie nodded her thanks and as she did, a massive pain flared through her head. She winced against it and instantly started massaging the area around her temples.

"You okay?" Ellington asked.

"Yeah," she said. "This headache…it's screaming at this point. I took some meds for it this morning and it's not touching it."

"Then get back to the motel and get some rest."

"It's one thirty in the afternoon."

"So?" Ellington asked. "Listen to me. I'm here now and these guys here at the PD are kicking ass. Go rest. I don't care if it's just an hour. You need to get some sleep. I promise you that I will call you if we find anything new. You have my word on that."

She would usually not even consider such a request— especially not when she felt that she was close to breaking a case. But this headache seemed to not be going anywhere and she knew if she didn't rest her eyes, it was going to get miserable quickly.

"You call me even with the *smallest* break," she said. "Swear it."

"I swear," Ellington said. He even held up his hand in a little mock salute, as if the other hand was on a Bible and he was in a courtroom.

He then leaned in and kissed her, right in front of the two officers that were still in the records room with them. It was a bit embarrassing, but it also meant the world to her. With a final gaze into his eyes, Mackenzie stepped away from the table and left the Belton Police Department.

Outside, walking to her car, she had to narrow her eyes. The glare of the sun was agony to her headache and right away, she knew she had made the right decision. It was not a decision she would have made on her own, helping her to realize just how much of an asset Ellington was to her. It made her feel foolish for being so ridiculously upset with him these last few days.

In the car, she pulled the sun visor down and sped back to the motel. She knew Ellington would remain true to his word and call her the moment he learned anything. It was with that assuredness that she headed back to the motel, looking forward to resting. Even if she could not fall asleep, the very act of just lying down in a dark room with her eyes closed would help the headache. She'd had them before and while they were a massive bitch to contend with, they could also be easily managed if she took the time to do so.

At the hotel, she popped two more ibuprofen, placed a Do Not Disturb sign on her door, and lay down. The pain still seemed to shred at the inside of her head. She used an old trick she'd heard about but never tried, getting a washcloth from the bathroom and soaking it in cold water. She rested it over her eyes as she rested and, miraculously, felt sleep rushing forward.

It came quickly despite the pain and although the headache refused to budge, sleep insisted itself upon her and within five minutes, she was out.

CHAPTER TWENTY SEVEN

Everything felt fuzzy when she woke up. She'd apparently not moved at all because the washcloth was still covering eyes. Only now, it was warm and drying. She waited for the shrill blare of her cell phone but did not hear it.

Weird, she thought. *Something woke me up. What was it?*

There was a smell, too. A scent that was sour in a way. Old. Maybe dusty and—

She reached up to move the washcloth from her face and that's when she heard the slight movement in the room. It was very soft, barely there at all. But it was close…damned close.

Her first thought was Ellington. Maybe he had come back to check on her.

No, he would have called. And he doesn't have a key. So how did he get in?

This was the thought that shook off the last vestiges of sleep. She opened her eyes as she removed the washcloth completely.

She saw the man, wearing a drama mask. And she saw the gun, close to her head.

She acted on impulse. She threw up her left elbow, connecting with the man's arm. The gun went off and she heard a ringing in her left ear at the same moment she felt an intense heat along her temple.

It took half a second to realize that she had been less than an inch away from death and in that half a second, she brought her left hand up quickly, curled into a U-shape. She struck the man in the throat and he made a gagging noise at once. He did not release the gun but he staggered back…and that was all Mackenzie needed.

From her lying position on the bed, she did a sort of half-somersault from the mattress, in the direction of the man with the gun. From the floor, she delivered a hard sweep to his ankle and he stumbled, nearly falling. As she did all of this in a very mechanical way, she also noticed that smell again.

Mildew? Dirt? Is he homeless, too…like so many of his recent victims?

As she carried out the action, a terrifying thought occurred to her.

I'm not hearing any of this. I haven't heard a damned thing since he fired that gun right by my head—a shot I can only assume was meant to go right into my skull.

As the man stumbled backward against the wall and the clunky air conditioning unit, Mackenzie reached up to the table all of her records and laptop sat on. Her Glock was there, holstered. She grabbed it and as she unholstered the gun, she charged the man, not wanting to give him a chance to rebound. She could not hear him gagging but saw his masked head hunched over; he was clearly still in some sort of pain.

Maybe I collapsed his trachea, she thought.

The man surged for the door and opened it. Mackenzie steadied herself, her nerves and the sudden jar from sleep making her shaky. As the man went out the door, she fired off a shot. She watched as the plaster from around the frame splintered, missing him in the shoulder by about two inches.

She did not hear the shot. Blind panic caused her heart to start thumping erratically. Still, she got to her feet and struck a crouching position. She wheeled around through the doorframe, onto the sidewalk.

She saw the man about ten feet away. He was facing her way, the gun aimed at her. Mackenzie fired at the same moment she fell back into the doorway. As she hit the floor, she saw the man's gunshot tear into the still-opened door.

I'm deaf, she thought. *That shot while I was in bed…it was too close. Shit.*

Near tears, she scrambled back toward the door, basically crawling on the ground. She dared another quick peek out of the doorway and saw him running across the parking lot, retreating. She took aim but her arms were trembling too much. Still, she fired. The only good it did was to scare the attacker as he dashed further across the mostly empty lot.

She let out a scream of frustration, torn between giving chase and calling for help.

It was not being able to hear that did it. If she went chasing after him and they got into some sort of hunt with one another, the loss of hearing would put her at a massive disadvantage.

She ran into the room and grabbed her phone. When she pulled up Ellington's number and called it, she could not hear the ringing. Crying now, she waited five seconds, giving Ellington enough time to answer, and started talking.

"I'm hoping you've answered this," she said. "He was here. The killer was here and he tried to kill me. Fired a shot for my head

140

and missed. But I can't hear...the shot was so close...I need you here. He's on foot, headed west. He left the parking lot about thirty seconds ago. Male in a costume mask, about six feet tall, average build."

A thought then occurred to her, one that made her both paranoid and afraid.

How the hell did he get into my room?

"I'm going to check the main office," she said. "Come quick."

She ended the call and placed the phone in her pocket. Then, still unable to hear and also unaware of a trail of blood slowly trickling down the left side of her head, Mackenzie sprinted outside, her Glock held down low, and headed toward the office.

***

She knew it was borderline irresponsible to go out into the open with her hearing shot. But she simply could not sit in the motel room and wait for someone else to come save her, either. She figured going to the office to see if her fears were true was a compromise.

As she neared the door, she kept her eyes on the parking lot ahead of her, making sure the shooter had not decided to return. With the coast clear and no one yet coming to see what the commotion of the gunshots had been about, Mackenzie reached the office door. When she pushed it open, she could tell right away that the news was not good.

There was fresh blood on the counter and the little pile of takeout menus on the right side of the counter has been knocked askew, some littering the floor. Mackenzie strafed behind the counter and found the clerk who had brewed her a special pot of coffee the night before lying in the floor with two bullet holes in his head, one of which had basically torn away the right side of his head.

A few of the drawers behind the counter had been pillaged through, one of which contained a collection of keys. She assumed the shooter had come in, demanded to know which room she was in while waving his gun around, and then killed the poor guy.

Without warning, Mackenzie felt as if someone had punched her in the stomach. It was hard to breathe and the world seemed to be spinning far too quickly. She stumbled back to the office door and as she leaned against it, she could blissfully hear something—though it was not a natural sound.

Rather than the presence of absolute silence, she could now hear a high-pitched ringing in her ears. And while this was beyond annoying and a little scary, she also knew that it was a good sign that the hearing loss was going to be very temporary.

Getting lucky on all fronts this evening, aren't you? she thought morbidly.

As she headed back to her room, a car came speeding into the parking lot. It came in so fast that the back end fishtailed a bit before it came to a stop several feet away from her. Ellington got out and came rushing to her. As he neared her, two police cars came into the lot behind him, their sirens flashing.

Ellington took her face in his hands and spoke to her. All she could hear, though, was the ringing.

"I can't hear you," she said. "He pulled the trigger right by my head, almost killed me. It's coming back though. There's a ringing...but forget that." She then pointed in the direction. "He went that way. And he killed the desk clerk."

Ellington turned back to the cruisers that had come into the parking lot. She saw Fredericks get out of one. He and Ellington spoke to one another and shortly after that, the driver of the other patrol car got back into his car and headed west, in the direction the attacker had retreated to.

Ellington said something else to her which she did not hear. He took her by the hand and led her back to the room. He eyed the bullet hole in the door uneasily before leading her to the chair beside the table. He then pulled out his phone and typed something into his Notepad app. He showed it to her when he was done.

You're bleeding. It's very little coming from your head. Other than the hearing are you sure you're ok?

She nodded. "I'm fine. Just scared the hell out of me. I...I was about a half a second from dying. One more inch...maybe even just half an inch..."

Ellington started typing again and showed it to her one more time. **So this means you can kick ass even in your sleep. Tell me everything that happened.**

She did her best to recount it all, from waking up to the softest sound and thinking it might be him. She was starting to tell him about finding the clerk in the office when Ellington gave her a *wait a second* gesture. He then reached for his phone, apparently answering a call. He sat down on the edge of the bed and began speaking to someone. He nodded a few times and then looked to Mackenzie, his eyes growing wide as he nodded again. He finished up his conversation and when he did, she was relieved to find that

142

she could hear the slightest murmur of his voice. She could still not make out any distinct words but it was much better than nothing.

"What is it?" she asked when he ended the call.

He typed some more and showed her the screen, which read: **That was Harrison. Some news. Also have some more that came in from the Belton PD when I was racing here. Really gonna make me type all of this out?**

"Yes," she said. "Please."

As he started, he stopped to go to the door where someone had apparently knocked. When he opened the door, Fredericks entered. They talked for a bit and moment by moment, the words became clearer. It was almost like hearing someone talk from underwater and then getting out of the water with her ears clogged up.

After a while, Fredericks finished up and headed back out. Ellington said one more thing to him, which Mackenzie could thankfully hear most of. "Just send the calls straight to me," Ellington said.

"I can hear again," she said when Ellington resumed his place on the edge of the bed. "It's murky but I can make it out. So save yourself the time…don't type anymore."

"Thank God," Ellington said. "Okay. So here we go…Sam Hudson, the vagrant that appears to be a local that ended up in Utah…he had three previous addresses. Two were in Belton and one was in Elm Branch. While in Elm Branch, he lived in your father's apartment building from 1982 to 1985."

"So that's another clear connection."

"It is. And you can add Jimmy Scotts to it as well. He lived there for all of 1985 before he moved out. All of that information came from the Belton PD. But then Harrison called the PD because they've been working great together today. Your father ran that building between June of 1984 and February of 1988."

"So the killer is targeting people that lived there while he did?"

"Seems that way. We're currently digging for information on Dennis Parks to confirm it. And the guys in Omaha are working hard as hell to ID more of the vagrants."

"But Sam Hudson…he had a kid. The kid didn't live there. He wouldn't even be born for almost twenty more years."

"Maybe he's gunning for family members, too. If he killed your dad because he happened to be the landlord, he could be coming after you because he knows you're his daughter."

"Or because I was getting close to busting his ass."

Ellington nodded. "Okay. So you only rested for about fifty minutes before some psycho tried putting a bullet in your head. How's the headache?"

"I don't even know," she said. "I'm too on edge about the last twenty minutes or so."

"I think you need to lay low. He knows where you are. He knows why you're here. If he took off on foot, he's screwed. They'll find him. This will be over in a few hours."

"We don't know that for sure."

"No, we don't. But I'm going to basically demand that you stay put for a while. I've already talked to Fredericks about it. He'll station a few guys outside of the room for you."

"I can't just sit here! He tried to kill me!"

"And he almost did. You have a headache that seemed to be killing you earlier and your hearing was compromised. All I'm asking is that you take a few hours. Hang out here and rest. And if you start looking through your files and laptop, I'll personally burn it all myself."

"No you won't."

He looked at her with all the sincerity he could muster. "No, I think I would. With the shit you've been through these last few days and not knowing where I stood with you...it's made me appreciate you on a whole new level. So yeah...if I had to destroy all this shit," he said, nodding toward all of the material on the table, "to keep you safe...yeah, I would."

She leaned forward and kissed him softly. "I love you," she said.

"I know you do," he said. "And I know how much it kills you to say it. So it's a good thing I love you, too."

She smiled at him and then looked to her watch. "It's two forty-five right now. I'll stay here and rest until four thirty. But that's the best you'll get from me. And during that time, I expect any updates as they come in."

"I can agree to that," he said. He then kissed her again and pointed back to the bed. "Rest. I'll see you in a bit."

They shared a warm glance as he made his way to the door and then he was gone again. As he closed the door, she noticed two patrol cars parked nose to nose in the parking lot—apparently sent there to keep an eye on her.

It made her feel like a child but after what she had just been through, she understood the need for it.

Besides...Ellington was right. She needed to rest. If she was being honest, she probably needed to see a doctor. The weight of

144

the headache still scared her and she had still not wrapped her head around the fact that she had almost died.

　　Rest, she thought. *That's not a problem...but there's no way in hell I'm sleeping now...*

CHAPTER TWENTY EIGHT

It was 2:47 when she lay down on the bed and by 2:50, she knew that sleep would be impossible. Still, it was glorious to lie down. She could feel the adrenaline wearing off as her body relaxed. The ringing in her ears came slightly for a moment and then died off. She had to lie down with her head at the foot of the bed to stay away from the hole in the mattress that showed where a bullet had nearly ended her life.

She kept replaying the scene in her head. She saw the man, slightly perched on the edge of the mattress. He'd apparently been bringing the gun down to her head when she had woken up. She guessed her sudden movement had distracted him just enough to buy her the half a second she needed to save her own life.

He'd been wearing the costume mask that the vagrants in Omaha had mentioned. She also recalled that they said he'd seemed like a fellow homeless person at first based on the way he had been dressed and seemed to know the area.

Maybe he'd just been scouting the area out, she thought. *If he is indeed killing people that lived in the same apartment building, he'd almost* have *to do some scouting. But one question remains: why wait so long between my father and Jimmy Scotts? Is there any significance to the timing of it all or has it always been random?*

And what would cause him to make the decision to kill these people? Was there some sort of perceived grievance on his end while he lived there? Or was there an actual event that occurred that he feels he needs revenge for?

There were too many loose ends to make sense of, especially with the headache and the coming and going of the ringing in her ears. She then went back to another thing that had never really sat right with her: the business card left in Wanda Young's mouth.

WELCOME HOME, AGENT WHITE.

Home.

It was a strange word in the context the killer seemed to use it. She had never looked back to Belton with any real sort of fondness. She actually hated to think of the place and it had depressed her a bit to come back here even for this case.

Maybe that had been his own morbidly poetic way of referring to Belton as his home, too. Had he been trying to tell them he was a local, trying to fill in the blanks for them?

But that smell on him. No...he's not a local. Not really. He smelled like someone who had been living on the streets. And if he lived on the streets here in Belton, everyone would know him—or about him, anyway.

Beside her, her cell phone buzzed with a text from Ellington. **Found a discarded gun in the woods about a quarter of a mile from the hotel. No prints but recently fired. Seems he ditched it and hid somewhere. Still haven't found him.**

He killed the clerk, she thought. *He was going to kill me. To do that, he'd have to have an escape plan...somewhere to go.*

She considered this, thinking that if Belton had the number of old decrepit buildings as Elm Branch had, he'd have any number of places to hide. But Belton was mostly open fields and forests. Surely he was hiding somewhere in the forest. And if that was the case, they'd have to bring bloodhounds in.

I'm missing something, she thought. *Something easy...*

She pondered it for a while, trying to make all of the pieces fit together into a picture that made at least some sort of sense.

He lived in my father's building while my father managed it. So far, it seems as if at least half of his victims did, too. Something happened to him there during that time...something bad enough that he saw fit to kill my father and all of those other people.

She thought of people living together in a building that small, compact, and close. She focused in on that and it was *that* train of thought that carried her all the way to 4:30 when the alarm she had set on her phone buzzed at her.

She sat up slowly and waited for her body to present itself with any complaints. The ringing in her ears was gone. The headache was still there, though it seemed mostly dormant. She did feel very tired but mentally sharp. Apparently, lying in the darkness and picking apart the details of a case that had been plaguing her for years was a great mental exercise—some sort of strange meditation in a way.

She texted Ellington with a simple message, trying to reestablish herself as in charge. **It's 4:31. I'm done. Where are you?**

He started responding right away. She saw the little dots in the display, telling her that he was responding. **At the PD,** he answered. **Trying to figure out where the gun came from. Come on down. There's coffee.**

You DO love me, she texted back.

She headed outside, nodded her thanks to the cops who had been watching over her, and returned to her car. The sun was still shining bright, reminding her that if the headache wanted, it could rear its ugly head at any time. For now, it seemed fine to stay at a low rumble in the back of her head. She figured she'd get as much done as she could before it changed its mind.

***

The coffee at the Belton PD was dark and good. There was also a sub platter, which she helped herself to right away, not realizing how hungry she was until she saw the meat and the bread. When she entered the records room and found Ellington with three other cops, she smiled at them all and asked: "Can we get the room for a minute please?"

The three cops seemed more than happy to take a break from poring over the files that were spread over the table. One of the cops was Officer Potter, the female officer who had accompanied Fredericks to her room last night.

Last night, she thought. *God, it seems like last week. I* do *need to get some sleep when this is over. Like vampire sleep...*

When Officer Potter closed the door, Ellington got to his feet and came over to her. He embraced her and kissed her on the forehead.

"How are you feeling?"

"I'm still tired," she said. "But I couldn't just do nothing."

"I know. But while these guys *are* busting their ass, there's nothing you can do here. It's either pore over the same files we've all been obsessing over all day or out hitting the streets trying to find this bastard. By the way, there has been a county-wide APB out for Greg Redman, and the main stretch of highway and three alternate routes have been closed on the outskirts of Belton and Elm Branch. If he was on foot when he left you, there's no way he made it out before the blocks were put up."

"So he's trapped somewhere in Belton or Elm Branch."

"Exactly. So there's really just the waiting. And as the great philosopher Tom Petty said, that's the hardest part."

"I say we hit the streets then," she said. "I can't sit down and stare at files anymore. After nearly getting my head blown off, I feel like I need to be up and moving around."

"Fair enough. But I'm driving. You look like hell."

"Thanks. Any luck on finding out where the gun came from?"

148

"No. But it is the same make and model that was used on every single victim to this point. Of course, there was no gun used on Wanda Young."

"Seems weird, huh?"

"A bit."

They made their way out of the records room and the headache startled to bubble up in her head. She almost willed it to go away and for a while, it worked. But then they were back out in the afternoon sunshine and she was reminded just how weak her sheer will was…in terms of the headache *and* this case.

I'm missing something obvious, she thought as Ellington drove them away from the PD and to the streets of Belton where there now seemed to be a police car on just about every corner.

She thought back to her reflection while resting in the motel room but there was nothing immediately apparent.

The gun? The mask? The latest business card with the message on the back? The smell? The desk clerk? The missing piece is somewhere in there. An answer staring me right in the face.

She looked out at the edges of the forest as they drove by it, the trees almost willed to grow between the buildings and houses. Knowing the killer might be out there, less than a few miles away, was infuriating. And with the fury that came with that, she was able to see past the headache and bring herself around.

WELCOME HOME, AGENT WHITE.

Welcome indeed, she thought. *Being in this town and feeling so trapped and frustrated, it's almost like I never left.*

CHAPTER TWENTY NINE

With connections being made at nearly every turn, it seemed to Mackenzie that things back in DC were now being kicked into high gear. Mackenzie continued to get real-time updates from what seemed to be an endless conference call where the identities of the vagrants were still trying to be determined.

At 7:35, Harrison contacted her to let her know that the name of another had been discovered: Aiden Biswell. Biswell had drifted all across America after dropping out of college in Texas in 1982. He worked small-town business and factory jobs until he dropped off the radar sometime in the late nineties. His name popped up all across America in police reports for petty theft and indecent exposure. He had last been sighted in Omaha in 2010 when a Good Samaritan had assisted him to the emergency room after he had been struck by a car.

"And here's the connection for you," Harrison said after giving the rundown on Biswell. "He was a resident of your father's building for seven months between 1985 and 1986."

It was the final nail Mackenzie needed. It was beyond coincidence at this point. She tried to dissect the meaning behind it as Ellington took them on their fourth circuit of Belton, in search of anyone who might seem even the least bit suspicious. She knew that there were bloodhounds that would be coming in later that night, trucked in from Lincoln. She also knew that even Kirk Peterson had been called in to help the police in their roadblocks and investigation. The final failsafe that had been set into place was, if the K-9 unit from Lincoln turned up nothing, a door-to-door effort would be kicked off early tomorrow morning.

All of that pointed to a solid effort and the end of the road for their killer. But still, Mackenzie's mind could not rest on those plans alone.

"Something had to have happened in that apartment building somewhere around eighty-five or eighty-six," she commented to Ellington. "Whatever it was, Greg Redman felt he was a victim of it. So if there's a police report, he likely wouldn't be listed as the guilty party."

"That's one of the routes Fredericks's men checked out today the moment we got Redman's name. He has no arrest record during that time. He *did* have one in eighty-one for getting involved in a bar brawl. He also had some marks on his record from high school for aggressive behavior."

Mackenzie had read all of that information as well—but it was all pretty common for people who eventually became murderers. The thing that really *didn't* fit in the case of Redman was that such a long period of time had expired between his first murder (her father) and his second.

"Maybe we need to start running arrest records on his victims," she said. "Maybe something *did* happen in the building but Redman wasn't involved. Maybe he just *felt* like a victim."

"That's a thought," Ellington said.

"Do me a favor, would you?" she asked. "Let's go back to the motel room. I keep getting this feeling that I'm missing something…something easy, right in front of my face."

"Something at the motel?"

"I don't know. I just…damn. This headache and being tired…it's making me feel stupid."

Ellington nodded as he cut a quick U-turn in the middle of the road. He flicked on the headlights, as night was starting to slowly descend upon the town.

"We need to check out that headache. I might force you to go to the doctor when this is all over."

She had been thinking the same thing. She'd experienced exhaustion headaches from time to time, but this felt different somehow. She wondered if it had gotten worse following the loud gun blast directly beside her head. If she was being truthful with herself, she'd felt a little off since she had narrowly escaped that encounter.

They were back at the motel ten minutes later. Mackenzie walked in slowly, cutting on the lights and looking around. She pictured the killer moving through the room, coming straight toward her with the gun in his hand. She sensed Ellington behind her, standing in the doorway.

"Is this one of those things where you need to be left alone?" he asked.

She only nodded, looking into the room.

"There are a few cops back at the office, doing clean-up from the scene with the clerk," he said. "I'm going to lend them a hand if I can. Let me know when you're good here."

Again, she said nothing. She looked to the bed, still untouched from where she had nearly been shot. Forensics had come in while she had been at the station with Ellington and had taken the bullet meant for her skull from the box spring, as it had torn through the mattress. They had also found two loose hairs, both of which were likely her own, but were still being tested. They were expecting results sometime early in the morning.

She began to walk around the room, from corner to corner. Now that she had a bit more insight into the killer, she was able to better slip into the way he might think.

A man with aggressive tendencies in his past. Something pushed him over the edge while he was living in a small, cramped space with at least one hundred other people. Killed once, very purposefully. Killed again many years later in a way that mimicked his earlier deaths. Left business cards to make sure we knew the deaths were linked.

It all added up to an uneasy answer. The killer was definitely unhinged but also very clever. More than that, he apparently took pride in the killings. He used those business cards to identify each of his victims as his own. And now that he sensed the endgame was near, he was getting even more brazen.

He had come into this very room with a gun, killing the clerk and just coming right in to kill her. *WELCOME HOME, AGENT WHITE...*

She sat on the edge of the bed and let out a heavy sigh. "What the hell am I missing?" she asked herself.

A bit shaky, she lay back down on the bed. She put her head where it had been when the killer had come in. She then closed her eyes and tried to picture her father in the same position. Asleep and unaware that someone was in the room. She then thought about the rest of the house while he had been sleeping...two girls asleep in their rooms, their mother on the couch. She then saw the house in its current condition, the brief walkthrough from the other day still fresh in her mind. The dust, the neglect, the snake in the cellar.

She then saw the man, his mask over his face. Looking down at her as if he did not fear her. The same man who had left all of those business cards. The same man who had killed her father.

WELCOME HOME...

Slowly, Mackenzie sat up.

The dust, the neglect, the snake.

The man on the bed, perched slightly on the mattress, the gun to her head. Blank eyes, a mask, the smell of dirty streets, of a homeless person...

Only, maybe that wasn't right. The smell had been noticeable, sure. But for a moment, she had almost recognized it as something else before she became aware of the danger of the moment.

The snake in the cellar...the smell.

With a gasp, Mackenzie got up from the bed, grabbed her Glock, and ran to the office to get Ellington.

It felt like a long shot...but there was something fitting to it.

It made a strange sort of sense.

Ellington saw her walking toward him and smiled at her. "You figured it out, didn't you?"

"I don't know. But I have a hunch."

"Do we need to call Fredericks?"

"Not yet," she replied. "I want to be sure first."

"Okay. So where are we going?"

WELCOME HOME, AGENT WHITE, she thought.

"To the house where I grew up," she answered.

CHAPTER THIRTY

Night had fallen when they pulled into the driveway of the house Mackenzie had spent most of her childhood in. At night, it looked very mundane, not even worthy of the memories Mackenzie still had of it. She opened the car door, staring at its murky outline against the backdrop of night. The forest behind it looked like some endless black sea that might swallow the whole place up at any moment.

"Now that we're here, will you tell me why?" Ellington asked.

"The card he left in Wanda Young's mouth said *Welcome Home, Agent White.* He's used those cards to claim each body. But with that message, he took a whole different step. And I apparently didn't figure it out fast enough—which is why he came to me and nearly killed me. I think he was telling me to come back here."

"Are you sure?"

"No. But when he was in my room, I smelled something. I thought it was just the man—that maybe he was homeless because some of the vagrant witnesses in Omaha stated that he looked like a homeless man. But there was something about the smell that I recognized. It's the cellar. When I came out here the other day, I went into the cellar. And it reeked. Mildew, dirt, rot, the smell of a place gone to waste."

"So you think he's hiding out here?"

"Maybe not at this very moment, but I do think he's been using it as a hideout of sorts since he came back."

"That's good enough for me," Ellington said, taking out his flashlight and aiming it straight ahead.

Mackenzie took out her own little Maglite as they walked across the lawn, their twin streams of light trailing side by side as they neared the porch. They took the steps up slowly, the creaking of their weight on them beyond creepy in the darkness.

Mackenzie tried to take the lead, heading for the door. But Ellington was having none of it. "Sorry," he whispered. "You almost died once already today. I'm taking the lead on this."

She wanted to argue her point but let it go. She enjoyed the feeling of being protected by him. And besides, he was right. She

154

was banged up and tired and probably shouldn't even be out here in the first place.

Ellington nudged the door open and stepped inside. Mackenzie followed behind him and was depressed to realize that it felt far too familiar to her. Like it or not, the empty spaces of the house did still feel like home in a skewed sort of way. Even in the dusty darkness, the place called out to her, luring out a few of the cherished memories of the house that had existed before the night she had found her father dead in his bed.

They made it through the living room and kitchen, finding nothing. They then ventured into the hallway. Ellington's light crept all the way down its length, coming to rest on the opened door of her parents' old bedroom.

As they headed down the hall, something in Mackenzie's stomach churned. Her arms broke out into gooseflesh and she could not deny that she felt like someone was watching them.

He's here, she thought. *This is it...this is where it's going to end.*

She thought of suggesting that they call Fredericks but ignored it. By the time they got back out to the car and placed the call they might miss their window. She was very aware of the feeling of momentum, of things surging forward toward...well, *something.*

They came to Stephanie's old room and found it empty. As Mackenzie looked inside of it, she felt tears stinging the corners of her eyes. These emotions had not been with her when she had been here a couple of days ago but now they seemed to be riding her back like a physical presence.

Her own room was next and once they swept their lights around the simple square space, she refused to look any farther. She was finding it hard to breathe and in the back of her head, she could feel the headache starting to rise, like a ride that was on its way to eat away at the shore.

"I don't know if I can do this," she whispered as Ellington came back out of the room.

"What is it?" he asked.

"I don't know," she said, though she wondered of this was what it felt like to have a panic attack.

"You need to go back outside?" he asked.

She shook her head. "Bathroom and then my parents' room," she said quickly. "Let's look in them and then get out of here. Some fresh air...then the cellar."

"Mac..."

"Just go," she said, nodding toward the end of the hallway.

155

With one final concerned look, Ellington checked the bathroom. Mackenzie stayed closely behind him, her hands clenching the flashlight and her Glock. She looked dumbly down at the weapon, not remembering when she had drawn it.

With the bathroom clear, that left only the room at the end of the hall. The room that had occupied her nightmares for so many years.

It doesn't matter, she thought as Ellington stepped through the doorway. *If Redman is here, he's in the cellar. He's waiting down there and—*

The sound of a gunshot broke that assumption apart. In the same instant, Ellington was partially turned around, slamming into the doorframe. Something warm and wet splattered against Mackenzie's face and left arm.

Ellington's flashlight went to the floor and there was a chaotic dance of light as he went down with it. Mackenzie dashed for the door, the Glock raised. She then watched as the shape of an arm came from around the side of the door. It grabbed Ellington by the shoulder and then the door was slammed closed.

"Open the door!" Mackenzie yelled. "Greg Redman, open the door now or—"

Her voice was interrupted by the sound of two more gunshots.

And a series of screams from Ellington that were cut short.

***

Mackenzie felt like screaming but managed to bottle it up. Tears flowed down her cheeks as she pictured Ellington dead in the same room her father had died in. She thought about simply throwing her shoulder into the door and letting herself inside. But she also knew that would give Redman a good two seconds to take aim and fire at her before she could properly orient herself.

No...he closed the door, she thought. *If he wanted me dead, he would have kept shooting after he took Ellington down. He might have tried to kill you earlier, but now he apparently wants to talk.*

Taking a deep, shaky breath, Mackenzie stepped toward the door. "Redman? What is it you want?"

"I want to be able to finish what I've been working on for twenty years," he said. "They all need to die. And from what I can see, the way out of Belton is blocked. And I need to get the hell out of here."

He spoke calmly, like a man who could not understand what the big fuss was all about.

156

"Did you…"

She stopped here, unable to get the question out. She bit back a sob and tried again. "Did you kill my partner?"

He chuckled again. "I don't think so. The bullet got him in the right side of the chest. The other two shots were just to freeze you."

"He's right," Ellington called out. "He's—"

His voice was interrupted by a loud clubbing noise, hollow yet metallic.

"Listen to me, Redman," she said. "If you—"

"That's funny," he said. "Your partner may still be alive, but I do currently have the gun to his head. You know the feeling well, yes?"

"All I was going to say is that if you let him live, I can get you out of Belton. I just need to know what it is you need to finish."

"I need to finish what I started with your father," he said. "I have a list, you know? There were thirty-five of them. So…well, I still have a lot of work to do."

"And what did these thirty-five people do to you?"

There was a pause here where she could actually hear Redman through the closed door, licking at his lips and breathing hard as he gathered his thoughts.

"They were in the walls," he said. "I heard them talking about me to each other. They made fun of me. They hated me. And your father was the worst of them. He had to be the first."

Mackenzie frowned as she listened. *That can't be it,* she thought. *I have not spent my life wondering about this case only to find that the killer is just insane. There has to be some other explanation. He doesn't appear to be schizophrenic…so why the hell would he kill all of those people?*

Still, she had to cater to him for right now and leave that mystery for later.

"These thirty-five people all lived in the building when you were living there?" she asked.

"No, not all of them. Some just came to visit, but they were just as guilty. Vultures. Rats. Always stealing my things. And then there was the little boy…the son of one of the people, a guy named Sam."

"Sam Hudson," Mackenzie said, recalling the name. "And you plan to kill the rest of them, too?"

"Yes. But it comes down to you. It's beautiful how history has brought us back together, don't you think? Like a circle…a perfect circle. One of two things will happen now, Agent White. You will kindly drop this quest you have to stop me and allow me to leave Belton. Once I am done—once I have finished my job—I will gladly turn myself in. I am not so far gone that I don't know that I must pay for these deaths."

"What's the second thing?" Mackenzie asked.

"You refuse and I kill your partner. And then you and I will just have to see who is more determined...see who will come out of this alive."

My father. Ellington. This fucking house...it's too much.

The headache roared in her head and it seemed as if the tears would not stop coming. Fully aware that she was pushing logic to the side and playing with fire, she responded with as much fear in her voice as possible. As she spoke, the sadness that had slowly started to envelop her morphed into a form of rage that, quite frankly, alarmed her.

He has a plan. If he thinks I'm falling into it, he'll become predictable. He thinks he's in control.

"I don't understand," she said. "You have killed all of these people just because they were mean to you?"

"Oh...much more than mean. They set out to destroy me. Whispering through my door at night, telling me all about the secret dreams I have. The dark, sick dreams. They knew me too well. They saw into my head, into my nightmares. They drugged me somehow...knew me inside and out."

Maybe it is *just a mental thing,* Mackenzie thought. *Maybe there is some sort of underlying schizophrenia...or maybe psychosis or some sort of blunt trauma to the head as a child...*

There had to be a better answer than this. She'd spent so much time...

"Will you help me, Agent White?"

"I'll do whatever I can," she said. "You took my father all those years ago...so please don't take my partner."

"I won't if I don't have to," he said. "Like the hotel clerk. I did not want to kill him. He was not one of the thirty-five. Neither was Sam Hudson's son. But I had to. So if I have to, I will kill this man, too."

"No...please...what do you want?"

"How many guns do you have on you?"

"Just one."

"I'm going to crack the door. Throw your gun in. I will then allow you inside and after I frisk you for other weapons, we're going to head out to your car. Just you and I, though. Your partner can stay here until I am delivered out of town."

"Okay," she said. "Just please take the gun away from his head."

"Not until you have been disarmed."

"Okay," she said, even throwing in a convincing whimper.

She waited, the rage boiling inside. It felt like a spring being pressed down and somehow fully aware that it would soon be released. The tension building, almost unbearable.

Redman cracked the door. "Throw your gun in."

Mackenzie did. At the same time, she stepped forward and placed her foot between the door and the frame. When Redman closed the door and it struck her foot, she lunged forward. Because he was closing the door, she knew exactly where he was located.

She felt him against her as she sprang forward. And although the door was between them for a moment, she was still able to throw her shoulder into his solar plexus. They both went sprawling to the ground, but as they went, she found his face with her right hand. She dug her fingers in, feeling his nose and his mouth. She dug her thumb into his mouth, refusing to let go.

His gun went off but she knew right away that it had missed her. The flash of it was to the right, a good foot away from her. They collided against the wall and she took advantage of the fact that he was pinned between her body and the wall. She drove her knee up into his crotch and as he hunched over, she grabbed his right wrist. She twisted hard, causing him to drop the gun. When it was dropped, she kept twisting, not stopping until she heard the crack of his wrist breaking.

He howled and bit down on her thumb, still in his mouth. She barely noticed it. She drove her knee into his crotch two more times and this time when he hunched over, he tried pushing back against her. But adrenaline and rage were controlling her to the point where it was almost like a blackout. As he pushed against her, she screamed and drove her elbow down hard into the back of his neck.

In most cases, this move was simply to temporarily stun or simply drop a perp. But she did it with such force and with such an aim that she was deliberately trying to cripple him. She wanted to hear his spine crack, to watch him fall in a heap, unable to move. While the move did drop him, he tried to attack back right away.

She stopped him with a hard kick to the side of his head. She heard something else snap—probably his jaw—and it only spurred her on. This time when Redman hit the floor, he did not try getting back up. He half-rolled into his side and in the weak slanted light of Ellington's dropped flashlight, she saw Redman's eyes in a daze.

No…not in a daze.

She also saw the blood come gushing out of his nose.

159

Redman was not blinking. He wasn't moving, wasn't breathing.

She'd seen this done before in videos, but with a punch that drove bone from the nose into the brain.

Apparently, it could be done just as easily with a well-timed kick to the face.

A sick satisfaction swarmed through her and then she fell to the floor beside Ellington. She wanted to look him over but she was blinded by tears and the headache that was even now surging forward like a stampede of beasts.

She felt his arm around her and his soft and gentle words.

"It's okay," he said. "It's okay."

But as she wept on the floor of the room her father had died in—the room that had haunted her for so long—Mackenzie didn't think anything would ever be okay. Because as Greg Redman had shown her, life was nothing more than a series of circles that looped back around on themselves.

Sometimes, those circles were individual wheels.

But more often than not, they got tangled up and were just waiting to snare those they had defined.

CHAPTER THIRTY ONE

Mackenzie White drank down her third margarita of the day and stared out at the ocean. She'd never been a huge fan of the beach but she did appreciate the cyclical nature of the tide and how no matter how far out to sea you stared, the horizon was unchanging, always there and permanent.

It also helped that this had been Ellington's idea, after McGrath had basically insisted that they each take two weeks off following the events in Belton and Ellington's subsequent recovery from the gunshot wound. Following McGrath's suggestion, it had taken Ellington less than one day to recommend that they get the hell out of Dodge.

So now here they were, sitting under the canopy of a beachside bar in Montego Bay, Jamaica. It was the fourth day of a six-day trip and she was already sunburned to the point of pain. Unlike most other pains she was accustomed to, though, this one was worth it.

Five weeks had passed since she had stepped out of her childhood home to a chorus of police and ambulance sirens. Ellington had been in the hospital for just a day and a half, as the shot Redman had placed on the right side of his chest had been high and cleanly passed through. Mackenzie, meanwhile, had recuperated in the comfort of her home, sleeping for chunks of time for about three days straight. The headaches that had assaulted her in Belton had continued to spring up, causing her to eventually head to a doctor. After an examination, he found nothing wrong with her but did offer one of two causes: high stress or exposure to black mold in one of the several abandoned buildings she had investigated while in Belton.

A week or so later, the headaches were gone and she had reported back to work. Which was exactly when McGrath had suggested that she take some time off. On the first day of her break, she had called Stephanie and her mother. She'd told them that the case was over, that the man who had killed their father and husband had been killed. Stephanie had asked for the grisly details but Mackenzie had not given them.

What she *had* done, though, was promise to visit both of them as soon as she was back from her vacation.

Only one other new item had come out of the follow-up investigations following the death of Greg Redman. During the time he had visited Nicaragua in 2003, a murder had occurred in the city of Managua. The victim was named Manuel Hernandez, and he had lived in America between the ages of ten and thirty-one. For a period of time between 1984 and 1986, he had lived in one particular apartment building in Elm Branch, Nebraska. As it turned out, there had been a business card on his body but when taken into evidence, it had been assumed to just be some sort of personal belonging. The business card had read Barker Antiques.

Four hours into their sixth day in Montego Bay, Harrison had texted Ellington—not going directly to Mackenzie at the order of both Ellington and McGrath. The text directed him to check his email and nothing more.

Ellington had left the beachside bar twenty minutes ago at this response and now, as Mackenzie started sipping on that third margarita again, she saw him coming back down from the condos above the beach. There was something both comical and sexy as hell about seeing him in Bermuda-style swim trunks and a tank top. He held a few sheets of paper in his hand and she promised herself that she would not punch him in the face if this was somehow work related.

"Was Harrison just jealous?" she asked. "Did he want you to reserve him a room, too?"

"No. And honestly, I called him when I went to the room to check my email. I chewed him out. But he had a good reason."

He slid the papers over to her as he signaled the bartender for another drink.

Mackenzie read the papers slowly, as the margaritas were catching up to her—and it was only one in the afternoon. Apparently, a lot of the requested paperwork from the State of Nebraska had just now come through. It was information that might have eventually helped in the Greg Redman case but would not have changed the outcome. Still, the missing pieces were good to have.

According to the report Harrison had sent over, the apartment building that her father had managed for a while had officially been condemned in 1994. The inspector who had made this call listed several reasons, including, but not limited to, water damage on the roof, weak joists, and a massive accumulation of toxic molds. There was even a small bit in the report of three different individuals who had tried to sue the building's last owner over medical bills related

162

to nausea, headaches, and vertigo that their doctors suggested could very well be the result of mold exposure.

Ellington had even gone through the trouble of underlining *toxic mold* and *headaches* for her.

Another document Harrison had sent over gave a brief explanation from an old toxicology report. It stated that certain neurological problems had been linked to the exposure of molds that contained mycotoxins, which could cause very severe reactions in the brain. These reactions could often lead to delusions, acts of aggression, extreme paranoia, and depression.

When she was done reading, she looked back out to the ocean and sipped from her drink.

"Harrison was quick to point out that no one is yet saying that this is the end-all-be-all explanation for why Greg Redman did the things that he did," Ellington said. "But it sure as hell seems to line up, right down to your headaches."

"I don't even know if I want an explanation," she said. "I thought there would be this sense of peace when I got the guy that killed my dad, you know? But there's nothing so far. And I'm afraid that getting an explanation is, to me, going to seem like the death of my father is being dismissed by Redman's psychological evaluations or, in this case, toxic mold exposure."

"I can understand that."

She smiled at him and took his hand. "You don't always have to agree with me."

"Oh, I know. But I also really *do* understand that. I watched you wrestle with this case since the day I met you—whether officially or unofficially. I'm very much glad it's over, too. And I don't want your pain to be dismissed, either. I've watched you wrestle with that, too."

"You have," she said, smirking. "Yet you stayed by my side. Even when I became kind of a cold bitch."

He kissed her softly. "Speaking of warm…I bet that water's fantastic. Want to go for a swim?"

"No," she said, sipping from her drink again and realizing it was almost empty. "What I want is for you to take me back to the room. And then after that, I want to come back out here, have about a dozen more drinks, and tell you about my family."

"Yeah?" he said.

"Yeah. I think after what you've been through at my side, it's the least I could do."

"The back-to-the-room stuff or telling me about your family?"

She gave him a playfully evil smile and took his hand, pulling him off of the barstool. "Both," she answered.

They exited the bar, leaving the canopy and venturing into the sunlight. A passerby who might have happened to see them dashing back toward the room, their hands all over each other, might have thought they were a young married couple on their honeymoon. It made Mackenzie feel lightheaded and a little immature. But that was fine with her.

She'd spent far too long trying to put her past behind her. And now that she had finally managed to step beyond it, unshackling herself from the chains and nightmares of her past, she was finally able to look into the future without reservation.

BEFORE HE PREYS
(A Mackenzie White Mystery—Book 9)

From Blake Pierce, bestselling author of ONCE GONE (a #1 bestseller with over 900 five star reviews), comes BEFORE HE PREYS, book #9 in the heart-pounding Mackenzie White mystery series.

FBI Special Agent Mackenzie White finds herself stumped. Victims are turning up dead, unrecognizable, their bodies hurled from the highest of heights. A deranged serial killer, obsessed with heights, is killing his victims from the highest locations. The pattern seems random.

But is it?

Only by entering into the darkest canals of the killer's mind can Mackenzie begin to understand what his motive is—and where he will strike next. In a deadly chase of cat and mouse, Mackenzie drives herself to the brink to stop him—but even then, it may be too late.

A dark psychological thriller with heart-pounding suspense, BEFORE HE PREYS is book #9 in a riveting new series—with a beloved new character—that will leave you turning pages late into the night.

Also available by Blake Pierce is ONCE GONE (A Riley Paige mystery—Book #1), a #1 bestseller with over 900 five star reviews—and a free download!

Blake Pierce

Blake Pierce is author of the bestselling RILEY PAGE mystery series, which includes eleven books (and counting). Blake Pierce is also the author of the MACKENZIE WHITE mystery series, comprising eight books (and counting); of the AVERY BLACK mystery series, comprising five books; and of the new KERI LOCKE mystery series, comprising five books (and counting).

An avid reader and lifelong fan of the mystery and thriller genres, Blake loves to hear from you, so please feel free to visit www.blakepierceauthor.com to learn more and stay in touch.

BOOKS BY BLAKE PIERCE

RILEY PAIGE MYSTERY SERIES
ONCE GONE (Book #1)
ONCE TAKEN (Book #2)
ONCE CRAVED (Book #3)
ONCE LURED (Book #4)
ONCE HUNTED (Book #5)
ONCE PINED (Book #6)
ONCE FORSAKEN (Book #7)
ONCE COLD (Book #8)
ONCE STALKED (Book #9)
ONCE LOST (Book #10)
ONCE BURIED (Book #11)
ONCE BOUND (Book #12)

MACKENZIE WHITE MYSTERY SERIES
BEFORE HE KILLS (Book #1)
BEFORE HE SEES (Book #2)
BEFORE HE COVETS (Book #3)
BEFORE HE TAKES (Book #4)
BEFORE HE NEEDS (Book #5)
BEFORE HE FEELS (Book #6)
BEFORE HE SINS (Book #7)
BEFORE HE HUNTS (Book #8)

AVERY BLACK MYSTERY SERIES
CAUSE TO KILL (Book #1)
CAUSE TO RUN (Book #2)
CAUSE TO HIDE (Book #3)
CAUSE TO FEAR (Book #4)
CAUSE TO SAVE (Book #5)
CAUSE TO DREAD (Book #6)

KERI LOCKE MYSTERY SERIES
A TRACE OF DEATH (Book #1)
A TRACE OF MUDER (Book #2)
A TRACE OF VICE (Book #3)
A TRACE OF CRIME (Book #4)
A TRACE OF HOPE (Book #5)

CPSIA information can be obtained
at www.ICGtesting.com
Printed in the USA
LVHW080802041019
633101LV00013BA/672/P